# Call Me Royal

CAROLINE BELL FOSTER

Editor: Tyrone Reid
Cover Design: Kevin at www.kgs.com
Author's Photograph: Brian Bell
Published by: Sunshine Publications
www.carolinebellfoster/sunshinepublications
ISBN-13: 978-0993067303

## ACKNOWLEDGEMENTS

I couldn't take the plunge and start this new venture without my college sweetheart Mr. Sunshine the man I freely give my heart. David thank you for supplying me with food when I forget and for keeping me grounded when I become to authorish.

Kyra & TJ your patience was noted and I apologise for the many times I've glazed over becoming lost in the world of make believe in the midst of our conversations around the dinner table.

To garner as much information about the Rastafarian movement there was only one place I would go and that is to the most famous Rastafarian family in Jamaica, thank you Donisha Prendergast for your endearing patience as I plied you with questions.

Rastarella Falade for being such a good friend.

## PROLOGUE

The dull tone signalling the arrival of yet another call sounded in Ingrid's headset. With bored automation she looked at the grey LCD screen on her phone, swiftly brought up the relevant order screen for the call on her computer and released the mute button on the black device connected to the phone. It all took less than two seconds.

"Thanks for calling QB, the quintessentially British company. My name is Ingrid. How may I help you?" She spoke in a voice one octave higher than her normal voice and devoid of her inner-city Nottinghamshire accent.

"Hello. I'd like to take advantage of the new customer offer please. The one for the Moped with the Union Jack on the front," the man on the line explained.

"Certainly, sir. I just need to take a few details from you and then we can proceed." Ingrid expertly switched to the personal details screen before continuing. "Have you an account with us, sir? Or may I take your name please?"

"Mr. Blue Knickers."

"I'm sorry, sir. I don't think I caught that." She adjusted the volume on her headset.

"Blue knickers, I like blue knickers," the man said in a harsh whisper. "What colour are you wearing, Ingrid?"

"I'm sorry, sir, but I do believe you dialled the wrong number, and I'll have to release this call. Goodbye."

Ingrid quickly pressed the release button with fingers that shook and punched in the three-digit code that let the floor captain know she had put herself on a personal and wasn't taking calls.

Every call, whether it was an enquiry, order, update, or complaint was given a three-digit code, and every time she wanted to give herself a moment to collect herself or even go to the toilet she had a relevant code to use. She hated it. She hated the hours she worked and most of the people she worked with, especially Fliss. But she was thankful for the money, and at least it got her out of the house and away from sticky jam fingers and beer cans five nights a week. She was thirty-one years old and stuck.

Chucking down her headset, she fluffed her hair and stood up. It was late, but the calls were too infrequent to make the shift pass quickly, and the hours were dragging. She still had eight hours to go.

"I just had a pervert again," she announced to her colleagues on pod eight who weren't on a call.

"What? Again?" said Della, the Jamaican Rastafarian. "This is what? The third time tonight?"

"Yeah. Why do I always get them?"

"I don't mind getting a call like that," Lucia, the beautiful language student from Spain on Della's other side, put in. "At least it breaks up the night and gives us a little excitement."

"Ooh, Lucia, the man is a pervert. He told me he likes blue knickers for goodness sake!"

"So what? I had him earlier and I said I like them too!" Della revealed. Those who weren't otherwise occupied laughed out loud and were glared at by those on calls.

"You're too much. You shouldn't encourage them!" Ingrid said sternly before ruining the effect by smiling.

"Ingrid, we do a twelve-hour shift. We need a little fun," Della replied, easing back into her chair.

5

They all laughed again.

"How come I never get a perv on the phone?" Mackenzie, the overly effeminate twenty-four year old, asked after pressing the mute button on his phone before going back to his customer.

"You really think a pervert wants to talk to a man? No way! No matter how pretty you sound on the phone!" Della teased throwing a paper click at the blonde giant who was sitting beside her.

"All of you are insane," Ingrid interrupted. "It freaks me out because I'm not expecting it, and he says everything with that posh upper class plum in his mouth." She shuddered dramatically. "I'm picturing him in a pinstriped suit behind a desk or something down in London."

"At this time ah night, Ingrid?" Della asked, standing up and stretching her arms above her head.

"He's probably making himself friendly with a certain part of his body. What do you call it?" Lucia asked. "Having a wenk?"

The whole pod erupted with laughter and those taking calls could clearly be heard apologising to their customers.

"You mean wank, Lucia," said Fliss, the more exposed of them all, though she was only nineteen.

"I agree," said Della, flicking a long ropey dreadlock over her shoulder. "I can see him now, sitting in his scruffy living-room with wood chip wallpaper and—"

"—and green shag pile carpet," Lucia added, before sitting down abruptly to answer a call.

"His mother is probably upstairs waiting for him to rub her feet!" Jarrett, the only alpha male, on the pod joined in.

"I bet he's never had a shag. A right old mummy's boy!" Fliss added with a laugh. "If I get him on the phone I'll ask him."

"Fliss, not even you can do that! You'll get fired if they hear you encouraging a call like that," Della warned.

"So?" Fliss replied, raising a thin eyebrow. "What is the first thing they tell us?" she asked, addressing no-one in particular. "Be polite to the customer and only ever hang up if they become abusive and you're offended. I can give as good as."

"Fliss, I can see why this is your what? Fourth job in a year?"

Fliss shrugged that I-don't-give-a-shit shrug she does so well. "Della, look at this place. It's a fucking dump! Why would I want to stay anyways?"

Della looked around, seeing the grey carpet stained here and there with coffee, hot chocolate or tea. The wonky vertical blinds with missing panels, grimy windows and walls painted in uninspiring beige. The entire floor was devoted to the night team and consisted of eight pods each sitting ten people. Two of the pods were completely empty and they didn't really talk to the other teams.

"Dump it might be, Fliss, but it pays my bills," Della replied just as a call came through and she sat down.

"If you get him again, Ingrid, transfer him over to me?" Fliss ordered, looking across at the older woman.

"No. I'll just hang up."

"You know what your problem is, Ingrid?" Fliss asked, her plucked eyebrows furrowing sharply.

"I'm sure you're about to tell me, Fliss," Ingrid answered warily. Everyone knew just how fiery and defensive Fliss could be and avoided an argument with her as much as they could. But just about anything could set her off. She was pretty in that milk and honey kind of way, but no-one ever saw past her foul mouth. "You're too fucking goody. Five kids and working in this—"

"Four actually."

"Four fucking kids, all under the age of seven, and working in this shithole. You're as fucking sad as the pervert!" Fliss shouted.

"That's not a nice thing to say, Fliss," objected Priya, the sole Asian on the pod, joining the conversation as she'd noticed the flash of hurt in Ingrid's eyes.

"What do you know?" Fliss glared at the other girl directly opposite her.

"I know you should apologise to Ingrid. You don't know anything about any of us," Priya challenged softly.

"Fuck you and Ingrid!" Fliss fumed. "As a matter of fact, fuck all of you!" Fliss swore loudly and without punching a code to stop all calls, flung off her headset, grabbed her lighter and cigarettes and stormed off. They all watched as she flung open the double doors at the other end of the floor and vanished down the stairs.

"That girl is full of so much drama," Mackenzie announced. "Not a night goes by without her having a go at someone."

"She needs to go to anger management," noted Della wisely, coming off her call. "But she's young."

"She and Priya are the same age," Ingrid pointed out.

"But Priya has lived a sheltered life. Fliss has lived more than even me. A druggie mother not much older than she is. She doesn't know her dad and she's resentful," Della said in her defence.

"That doesn't give her the right to talk to people the way she does though Della," Mackenzie said.

"She's lived a hard life, Mac, and is looking for an identity for herself. Half white, half black is not easy and even harder when the white side doesn't like or understand the black side of herself," Della explained in an accent dipped in patois.

"You think that's what it is?" Ingrid asked.

"I know so. She's really hard to like. But can you imagine twelve hours without her swearing and saying 'I need a fag' every five minutes?" Della chuckled. "She definitely livens up the place."

"Come on. It's almost time for a fag break," Lucia announced and then slapped her hands over her mouth in horror when she realised what she'd just said.

They all laughed.

## CHAPTER ONE

Della tapped her living-room window twice before unlocking the front door. She lived in the old part of The Meadows within walking distance of the Embankment and the river Trent. In the summer, every house on her street had a pretty window box overflowing with flowers, but hers was the only one that had a wooden door and brass door knocker, a handle and number she polished every week. The houses dated back to the 1800's.

Giving Mr. Motive a chance to move away from the door, she still had to bend and scoop him up with one hand as he slept just inside the doorway. He'd make a perfect kitty drought stopper if he ever managed to stretch full length, she thought, scratching his ear.

Careful to take her shoes off while still holding the cat, she placed them neatly on a mat just for that purpose and stepped into her bright pink novelty slippers. She entered the white-on-white living room she never used, and headed for the back room she used for everything. She dropped the cat on the sofa, put her bag on the bare wooden floor and walked through to the very narrow galley kitchen to make herself a pot of tea and a sandwich.

This was day three of a four-night stint, and she was feeling exhausted and old. At one time she could go several nights without feeling tired. Now she struggled past the second night, but the money was too good for her to change jobs. She needed every penny.

Reaching for her tea-for-one teapot set she'd received as a Christmas present from Monica-Louise one year, she made a cheese and tomato sandwich, opened two bags of plantain chips and poured them onto a plate. Closing her eyes, she reached into her jar of surprises and pulled out a chocolate bar and put everything onto a tray and walked into the living room.

Mr. Motive, used to the ritual, waited for her to turn on the TV and settle down before he curled himself into a tight little ball beside her, one white paw touching her thigh possessively.

*** 

Make sure to tidy your desks and put everything away," Monica-Louise said as she circled the pod, picking up empty plastic cups and odd bits of paper.

"Why? What's going on?" Jarrett asked in his deep Nigerian accent.

The floor captain moved to his section and rested her hip against the empty desk beside him. "I got an e-mail advising the directors may come in tonight."

"Tonight? What for?" It was already after eleven.

"To meet us. Apparently our new chief from down in London dropped by unexpected and the whole place was a mess." Monica-Louise stood up dusted the thin layer of dust from her black trousers and straightened the keyboard before moving away again.

"Sounds fishy to me. I've been here for years and never yet seen none of them big fish come at dis time ah night. They're going to get rid of us."

"They can't get rid of us Della; we keep the place running," McKenzie stated confidently.

"Then why come?"

"Just to say hello? Who knows," McKenzie shrugged as he

removed the single earphone to his mobile from his ear. Listening to music throughout the night helped him concentrate, he always said. But normally audio players weren't allowed on the floor.

Della kissed her teeth suspiciously but said nothing more. They were lucky to see a manager, even when they were leaving in the morning. No, something wasn't right, she thought, but kept it to herself.

"Right, before another call comes through put yourselves on meeting, and put all your belongings in your lockers. Including your phone, Felicity!" Monica-Louise ordered as she watched the younger girl hide her phone under a folder. "The only things on your desk should be the current winter catalogue," she warned. "And, Mackenzie, take that photo of yourself down as well." She organised as she picked up the newspapers she'd been collecting from the pods and dumped them in the already overflowing recycling bin.

*** 

Another forty-five minutes elapsed before four men in dark suits walked onto the floor and, as curious as the rest of them, Della turned to see the men who held her future in their hands. She needed this job.

One was a typically stocky no-neck type with sparse hair. She'd seen a picture of him before in the company newsletter, but she simply couldn't remember his name. Then there was the hunky blonde who looked to be in his early thirties. He had bossy ambition stamped all over him with a toothy grin and a sheen of sweat on his forehead. A pale, fragile-looking man stood to one side. The fourth man was well-built but in profile to her.

Della watched with a sympathetic shake of her head as Monica-Louise rushed over to meet them, gushing over the introductions and doing an impressive amount of preening and hair flicking.

Hearing the beep in her headset, Della reluctantly turned away from her entertainment for the night and concentrated on the call.

\*\*\*

It had been a long day that had started with his youngest daughter, Gabbs, dramatically flinging herself across the bonnet of his BMW with all the drama and mutiny of a teenager about to embark on the second day of punishment. She was grounded, and Spencer had also confiscated her phone, laptop and keys and banned all her friends from coming around. Gabbs was getting out of hand and he was getting desperate. But Spencer had hardened his heart against the tears and when she got into the car and buckled herself in, he decided to have a little fun. It had been months since any of his daughters had spent any one-on-one time with him, and now that Gabbs was in the car wearing furry bear-claw slippers and a faded onesie, he decided to make the most of it.

Spencer had planned on going on a quick drive, taking her out for breakfast and having her home before his scheduled nine o'clock meeting. Problem was, he'd taken a wrong turn and found himself on the M1 heading North.

It was midday when he came off the motorway at Junction 25 and found himself in the East Midlands closest to Nottingham.

He'd pulled over when it was safe to do so and called his PA to let him know he'd be out of office. Then he finally turned on the Sat Nav and headed into the city. Much to his Gabbs' horror, he decided to stay in Nottingham for a couple of days, with plans to see the new company they'd just bought and spend some time with her.

He'd visit QB first to get it out of the way. Then he'd be all hers, he promised. That suggestion was met with a blank stare and folded arms. Gabbs could do silent stubbornness very well, and when he could no longer endure her sulky glare, he relented and gave her his credit card and her phone and told her to buy them both some clothes. He chuckled at the way she pounced on her phone, as though she'd been starving for oxygen the whole time. Teenagers!

So here he was, stuck in a bloody circus of bowing and scraping and eager introductions made by awe-struck employees and department heads, all of whom, he assumed, were now wondering if their jobs were at risk.

## CHAPTER TWO

The eighth floor was a depressing place, Spencer thought to himself, as he looked around surreptitiously, mentally documenting and quickly calculating the cost of refurbishment. The company couldn't ask their employees to give top customer service if their working environment looked as drab and uninspiring as this.

He'd seen it a million times before, with twenty-four-hour call centres offering a worldwide service, and had experienced it first-hand himself when he'd worked the night shift at a telephone company during his stint at university. He'd start his shift and see remnants of celebratory cakes and stale sandwiches on foil platters and then group emails telling everyone to help themselves as the company celebrated a target win or a new contract. It was demotivating. Yet he knew this lot hit their targets with ease but were obviously undervalued. He wanted to change that.

Spencer allowed himself to be herded along with the other execs past several pods until they were standing by a group of desks in the centre of the floor, where the curvy blonde proceeded to go into minute detail about the workings of her team.

Spencer switched off. He really needed to get back to Gabbs before she bought the hotel and the latest gadget. What had he been thinking giving her his credit card like that? Nicole, her older sister, had never given him this much agro. But, then again, she went off with the first boy she'd brought home and moved out. Then there was Jesse, his errant middle child, who took off with a backpack three months ago. Last destination, Kenya. He loved his daughters but they were turning his hair grey.

Hearing a tinkle of laughter he'd know anywhere, Spencer froze and things literally moved in slow motion as he turned slightly to find its source.

He hadn't heard it in twenty-odd years, and hearing it now brought a wealth of feelings that burned his chest. Was it anger? Yes. Was it pain? Yes. Was it hate? Definitely.

Scanning the pod nearest to him, he saw her and pinned her in place with a stare. The bitch.

She'd changed almost beyond recognition was his first thought. She looked a lot older than he remembered. She was hunching over the desk in a way that would no doubt be detrimental to her back and shoulders a few years down the road. She'd put on weight. Lots of it.

She wore a thick black jumper and long earrings that had shells on the ends. It was the type of jewellery Jesse now wore. Her hair was upswept and wrapped around her head like a turban. A turban of dreadlocks. What the hell, dreadlocks? She'd become a Rastafarian? Little shells dotted her hair here and there. She looked far from the sophisticated, confident women he'd known back in Jamaica when they were kids. This Della looked tired, old and worn out. What the hell had she been doing with her life! He felt a stab of sympathy, as this was not how he expected her to be. And this was the last place he expected to find her working. But never mind all of that, he thought, as he shook his head slightly to clear it. He wasn't going to look back. He wanted her gone.

Della dipped low in her chair. When the men walked by, she knew it was Spencer. He looked exactly how she knew he would. Taller, stronger and even more beautiful. He'd been a cute kid, all dimples and huge dark eyes. He'd been gangly and handsome at thirteen and never suffered from the pimple phase everyone else had at eighteen. He was beautiful, and she felt breathless excitement skittle down her spine. Spencer was here, just twenty feet away.

She glanced up again and felt his dark eyes lance through her the way they'd done all those years ago. He still hated her. Knowing she had a half-hour break coming up, she knew she was going to run, hide, whatever. But she wasn't about to sit here feeling all exposed and vulnerable, waiting for him. She wasn't ready for this. Another lifetime and she still wouldn't be ready.

Finishing her call and not even knowing what the customer had ordered, she punched in the break code, picked up her door pass and, with head held high, left the floor.

Spencer watched her go and barely managed to smile and nod his way through more introductions before excusing himself and walking out. He'd been rude. But he was mad. Damn mad. How dare she walk out on him. Again. Her back ram-rod straight, just as it had been that night. He was angry, hurt and wanted an explanation, but by the time he made his way down the stairwell, Della was long gone.

Della walked straight out of the building, through the car park, barely glancing at the bulky cars that weren't normally there, and marched up the street. She had thirty minutes to figure out what this meant. She went into Franco's, the small all-night café that catered to shift workers, and ordered herself a mint tea from Franco then immediately cancelled the order and ordered a black coffee instead. She'd need caffeine, even if it was cheating.

What was Spencer doing in Nottingham? What did this mean? He clearly didn't know she worked there, as he seemed just as shocked as she was for a split second before he straightened his back and glared at her from across the room.

She knew he was going to come over to her. That's why she'd practically ran out. She did not want him to question her in front of her colleagues, and she did not want the resurrection of her past to be witnessed by her friends.

What was Spencer doing in England anyway? He was supposed to be living in Jamaica or maybe Miami, but not here. His family had no influence in England. His surname would not open any doors here. Chandler-Wright meant nothing.

She had so many questions to ask. Why now after all these years? She wasn't ready for this. Her life was okay. She was fine.

She shouldn't have left the office though. That was now the problem. She should have stuck her hand out, shook his and pretend that she didn't know him. Yes, that's what she should have done. No, who was she kidding? She wasn't a teenager anymore, and neither was he. She never did play those teenage games. But maybe if she did, they wouldn't have ended up in such a damn mess. She hadn't been home in twenty-odd years, thanks to him. He had no right being in England. This was her country!

Seething but focussed, she finished her coffee and walked out with a wave to Franco. She'd pay him later.

It was drizzling and the night air was cold. If she got even a sniffle it would be Spencer's fault. The car park was now empty.

Using her card, Della swiped the reader. The light on the metal plate turned green to release the lock. She had two minutes to get to her desk and sign in. It normally took her four minutes just to sign in. She was going to be late. She was never late.

You missed it all, Della," Felicity declared, as soon as Della sat down and lifted her headset.

"Never mind. Maybe next time."

"Don't you even want to know what they were like?" asked Felicity.

Realising it would seem odd if she didn't show even a little interest, Della relaxed into her seat and forced a smile at Felicity, who was standing up and peering intently at her.

"Are we fired then?"

"They were all right, Della. Especially the new guy. He was lovely, asking all sorts of questions as though he was really interested."

"That's nice. So we nah get fired?" she repeated with a tinge of patois. Her accent always came out when she was emotional.

Felicity laughed. "Fuck no. He even noticed how dated our headsets were and said he'd look into getting us some wireless ones!"

Della felt sick. She wanted to curl up into a tight little ball and cry. He was still caring and nice. He always had been. Completely different from the rest of the Chandler-Wrights.

"Good-looking man he was," Ingrid said, joining the conversation. "He stood right at your desk, Della, and fiddled around while he talked to us."

Della immediately scanned her desk to make sure there was nothing personal on it.

"What was his name again? Steven something or other."

"Spencer Adam Chandler-Wright," Della answered automatically. She looked up from her screen, feeling two pairs of eyes on her. "What?"

"You know his name?" Ingrid asked, sounding confused.

"His whole name?" MacKenzie stressed with a jaunty look.

"Cho, man. I did google him and it came up," Della lied quickly. She then pretended a call had come through and started talking to no-one.

*  *  *

Gabbs hadn't done too badly, Spencer thought, as he glanced at the clothes hanging in the wardrobe. She'd bought enough essentials to get them through the next few days, even the lemony shaving foam he favoured.

After taking a quick shower, he pulled on the white t-shirt and navy sweat bottoms she'd bought and slipped on a pair of slippers before walking into the main sitting area of the two-bedroom suite.

Gabbs was curled up in the corner of the large sofa, her mass of brownish blondish hair piled on top of her head as she watched a music channel. She was wearing clothes identical to his. He smiled.

Of his three daughters, Gabbs was the most affectionate and open.

He was glad he'd decided to stay, instead of racing back to confront Della. Della wasn't going anywhere. His relationship with his daughter was going through a transitional phase, and he was well aware that he had to tread carefully. Making a wrong move, he could lose her like her sisters. A complicated girl, Gabbs darted from childlike petulance to defiant teenage angst to displays of maturity within minutes of each mood swing.

Getting a cold beer from the mini fridge, Spencer settled in beside her and pulled her into the crook of his arm. It was just the two of them at home now. They hadn't done this in months, and he felt guilty.

"What you watching, Fuzz?"

"Seriously, Dad. Fuzz?"

"What? I've always called you Fuzz," Spencer replied, as he pinched the remote from her hands.

"I'm almost seventeen, Dad, practically a woman." She grabbed the remote from him and sat on it.

Spencer managed not to choke on his beer. "Women don't do what you did the other night, Gabbriella," he reminded her. "The police, Gabbs? What were you thinking?"

"You're not about to go into lecture mode are you, Dad? Cause I've just about had enough of this whole punishment stuff. How long are you going to keep this up for anyway?" she whined.

"Never mind that. Look, Gabbs." He turned slightly so that they were now facing each other. "Put yourself in my shoes for just a sec." She pulled out of his arms. "What are you doing?" he asked, as she used her bare feet and toed off his slippers and put them on instead.

"OK," he chuckled. "You're in my shoes. You send me a text telling me you're staying the night at Michelle's house—"

"Malina's," Gabbs interrupted.

"Malina's house. Then the police are at my door at four o'clock in the morning." He paled as he recalled that night, thinking something had happened to one of his girls. Then Gabbs had stepped from

19

behind the police officer with fire in her eyes. She wasn't at all sorry then. "How would you feel?"

"I'm sorry, Dad," she whispered, looking down.

"The only reason they brought you home was because one of the officers recognised you from a charity event we went to last year!"

"I know, Dad," Gabbs said, starting to sob.

"You stole a car!"

Tears rolled down her cheeks and dripped off the end of her nose. He pulled her close again and kissed the top of her head. It had taken three whole days for her to be truly contrite.

"We won't talk about it anymore, okay?"

"Okay." Gabbs smiled through her tears and wrapped her arms around her dad's neck. "Can I get all my stuff back?"

"No."

"Dad!"

"No."

"Okay."

They remained silent for a long time.

"I've missed this, you know, Gabbs," said Spencer, finally.

"Yeah, me too. You're always at work."

"It's what I do. A lot of people rely on me."

"Yeah, but what about me, Dad? You're never home."

"So this last little stunt of yours was to make me sit up and take notice?"

"Will you be mad if I say yes?"

He sighed. "I noticed Gabbs. But next time you do something like that I'll send you to your granddad's in Jamaica, and he can deal with you."

"No way, Dad!" She pulled out of his arms to look at him, her eyes wide with horror. "I'd rather stay with Miss Daphne, the lady next door. She's lovely and makes the best sweet potato pie. Lush."

Strange, Spencer thought. For years he'd neither seen nor heard from Della, and now his daughter talks about her mother being lovely.

"Her daughter works at QB," said Spencer.

"Really? Wasn't she your girlfriend or something? I heard—" Gabbs stopped abruptly and bit her lip, as though physically stopping the words from tumbling out.

"You heard what?"

"I'm being brave now, Dad, so don't be mad." She took a deep exaggerated breath. "I heard Granddad gave her money to go away."

"Who told you that?"

"One of Granddad's staff," she admitted. "Well, is it true? Cause Miss Daphne doesn't talk about her at all, and I haven't seen any pictures of her either. What's her name anyway?"

"Della."

"Stupid name. What did she do when she saw you?" Gabbs was on a roll. "Fall at your feet and beg forgiveness?"

"You read too many novels," he grumbled. "She ran," he admitted reluctantly.

"Ran! Ran where?"

"She just took off." He rubbed his hand over his face. "I don't know why I'm even telling you this."

"Cause you love me, and we're close."

"Hmm."

"Did you go after her then?" Gabbs was literally sitting on the edge of the sofa in anticipation.

"I did."

"Oh wow, Dad." She clasped her hands to her chest. "You went after her. That's so romantic. What happened next?"

"I didn't find her."

Gabbs looked crestfallen. "I'm sorry, Dad," she said, snuggling to his side again. "We can try and find her tomorrow."

"I can, yes."

"I won't be staying in this hotel all day tomorrow though, Dad."

"That reminds me. Credit card, please."

The pout came back.

"And the laptop."

So did the glare.

"I'll let you keep your phone."

Gabbs smiled and gave him a squeeze. "Love you, Dad."
"Rightbackacha, Fuzz. Let's watch a film."
She gave him the remote.

## CHAPTER THREE

"Listen up, you lot." It was the start of the night shift, and Monica-Louise was standing beside their pod with a look of excitement on her overly made-up face. "Mr. Chandler-Wright wants to meet you all on an individual basis," she said. "Felicity? Starting with you. He's in Conference Room 2 upstairs."

Della hadn't slept all day and had almost rung in sick, but finally decided that Spencer Chandler-Wright was not going to make her lose this month's commission because of a sick day. It was too late in the month and she'd earned too much.

Felicity returned not five minutes later with a smile on her face.

"What did he say?" Mackenzie asked as she settled down.

"Not a lot really. Asked if I liked it here and if there were any changes I would like to see, and if I'd be interested in joining one of the company's work-and-learn programmes."

"And what did you say?"

Felicity was about to reply but was stopped by the approach of the floor captain.

"Mackenzie, you next, then Ingrid, Priya, Jarrett, and then you Della," Monica announced, pointing at each of them in turn.

Della would have preferred to go now, as she felt like the only duck in the pond during hunting season.

"You're next, Della," Monica-Louise called out sometime later and, looking at her screen, added, "and you may as well take your first break right after."

Della nodded her thanks and walked very slowly up to the next floor and dithered in front of the closed door.

"Get in here, Della," Spencer called out, making her jump. She squared her small shoulders and marched in.

She didn't look any better than she had the night before, Spencer noted grimly. Same long black skirt, same thick black jumper, but her dreadlocks were loose, reaching past her waist. Her earrings were large pearlescent shells that reminded him of a full moon.

He moved around the massive square desk that could seat forty people comfortably and stood in front of her and looked down. She was tiny, yet he remembered a time when she was taller than him and able to climb over the fence that separated their properties, while he had to suffer the indignity of crawling under it. He was six months older than she was, and she'd hated it.

"Aren't you going to look at me?"

Della reluctantly raised her head and looked at him. "It's good to see you, Spencer." He was dressed casually tonight. Dark blue jeans, light grey shirt and a black jacket.

He laughed. At least she remembered his name.

"I'd like to say the same, but I can't." He moved away, crossing the room to sit far away from her. He'd always wanted to wrap her up in his arms whenever she was near and, damn it to hell, he still did. "What are you doing here?" he asked.

He picked up a pen and began fiddling with it.

"You wanted to see us," Della said.

"That's not what I'm talking about, and you know it!" he growled roughly. He rocked back in his chair and then moved to the window, looking at the empty road below. He didn't know what to say. There was so much he wanted to ask her, but for some reason felt almost afraid of the answers she would give. "And sit down for god's sake!

You're standing by that door as though you're ready to bolt or something!"

Della was about to shout back, but changed her mind. Instead, she pulled out the nearest chair to her and sat down.

"I'd like to say that you look well, Della, but you don't."

"If that was meant to hurt me, you made a mistake. You can come better than that."

"Oh, I mean everything I say. I'll leave all the lying up to you!"

"What do you want from me, Spencer?"

"An explanation as to why your mother hasn't seen you in years for one," he drawled. "How could you do that to her?"

"It's none of your business."

"You're her only child, and she's pushing seventy. She's all alone—"

"Alone?"

"She's rattling around in that huge house with only a paid companion for company," Spencer seethed. "Since when did you become so hard and unfeeling?"

She stood up and faced him. She was not going to be made to feel guilty here. It was all on him and his family.

"I don't want to talk about my family to you. I work here. Do I still have a job?"

"I could fire you."

"You could, but you won't."

"You're right, I won't. I'm not the cold, heartless one in the room right now, am I?"

Della sighed. "Look," she said, rubbing her eyes. "I'm tired and this is the last night of a four-night rota. I can't do this right now."

"When then? We have to talk."

"Why, Spencer? We were kids. We fell in love and right back out of it when things got a bit complicated. We're adults with responsibilities now."

"You're not married."

"How do you know that?"

"I asked around."

25

"Why am I not surprised you using your name to get what you want," Della replied bitterly.

"Actually, I simply asked Ingrid," Spencer confessed. "She was very forthcoming." He moved a little closer. "So what responsibilities do you have? A lover?"

She lifted her chin. "A mortgage. Bills. Life."

"How long have you lived up here?"

"Here Nottingham or here England?"

"Both."

"Nottingham seventeen years and England a couple of months after your eighteenth."

"Really?" Spencer frowned.

Della hadn't intended to reveal so much and could see him trying to remember the details of that time.

"It was a long time ago," she whispered. She didn't want to remember, and she didn't want him to start asking her questions about that time either.

"Yes it was," he answered vaguely with a far-away look in his eyes.

"Do I still have a job?"

His forehead creased in irritation. She was hung-up on a job she was overqualified for. He knew Della could do the job with her eyes closed.

"Yes you do. I wouldn't fire you; you make me money," Spencer joked.

Gasping, she pulled herself up to her full, unimpressive height of five feet two inches. "Yes, it did always come down to money. Didn't it, Spencer? Any how, any way."

"Where do you think you're going?" he asked as Della moved to the door.

"It's my break time."

"I haven't finished with you yet." He moved quickly around the desk and leaned against the door with his arms folded across his chest before she could leave.

"Spencer, stop the game playing. You can't keep me locked in your office. I'm an employee."

"Want to bet. What's with the heavy patois and the dreadlocks?"

"What?" she asked, completely thrown by his question.

"The patois. You don't speak like that normally. You never did, your mother—"

"Let's leave my mother out of this. Are you going to let me pass?"

Della noticed the playful glint in his eyes. Spencer had always been playful. His brother less so.

"How's Jeremy?" she asked and watched the spark die from his eyes as she knew it would.

"It always came back to Jeremy. Didn't it, Della? You never could make up your mind which one of us you really wanted. But having sex with both of us was surely a bit risky for a church-going girl like you."

Della gasped. After all these years, it still hurt that he could even believe such a thing. That's why she didn't want to talk to him. It brought back things she didn't want to think or talk about.

"You're putting yourself at risk, Mr. Chandler-Wright," she scoffed. "Keeping me in this room, just the two of us, the door closed. I could scream rape and the whole Chandler-Wright dynasty tower of fame would come tumbling down like a pile of bricks."

He was silent for a moment, just looking at her with his dark eyes, trying to figure her out.

"Go on, touch me, Spencer," she spat as he reached for her. "And I swear to God I'll scream this place down."

He dropped his hand and shook his head, as though unwilling to believe she would falsely accuse him of something so sordid. What had happened to her? They used to be friends. Lovers.

They stared at each other, Della's eyes dark and stormy, his confused and hurt. He moved aside to let her pass. Stopping in the doorway, she turned to him. "Happy birthday."

# CHAPTER FOUR

He was surprised to see where Della lived. In Jamaica, her parents' home was a huge three-story monstrosity with lots of balconies and windows with green awnings. Della's house in comparison was small and narrow with one door, a sash window beside it and another sash window upstairs.

At Gabbs' suggestion he'd brought breakfast with him. Gabbs thought she was helping in his quest for love. If only, he thought mockingly.

Spencer knocked on the door and waited impatiently. The door opened to reveal a very unwelcoming Della, with arms folded arms and a rigid stance. It was a little after nine and she was still wearing her work clothes.

"What do you want?" She didn't bother to ask him how he knew her address.

"I brought breakfast." He hoisted the two plastic bags and stepped into her house with one smooth move. He gazed around in surprise. The room was stunning in a don't-sit-on-the-sofa kind of way. All white, even the carpet was an impractical shade of white.

"Guess you want me to take my shoes off, huh," he asked ruefully.

Della pursed her lips and watched as he toed off his loafers and placed them with exaggerated care onto the mat beside her shoes. The twinkle was back in his eyes, she noticed. She wasn't in the mood for a playful Spencer. Hell, she didn't want Spencer here whatever his mood.

He was dressed in black jeans, a collarless mustard shirt, and a black leather jacket that looked soft, expensive and new. Della didn't offer to take it from him.

She led the way through the living room, through the back room and straight into the kitchen. Her tea-for-one set was at the ready and she looked longingly at her jar of surprises. She was in desperate need of a sugar fix.

"Would you like a cup of herbal tea? I have mint or chamomile?" she asked, now resigned to the fact that he was here and they were going to talk whether she wanted to or not.

"Mint please." Spencer couldn't stand the whole herbal foolishness but didn't want to put her out. He could see the strain in her eyes and felt a tug of remorse. He knew that they were going to have to talk at some point, and it probably wasn't going to be pleasant.

"Let's make a deal," he suggested, putting the bags down on the counter beside her and shrugging out of his jacket. He pitched it through the doorway. It landed on a nearby chair. "We used to be best friends. Let's try and remember that and just enjoy breakfast, okay?"

"Humph." Della made a sound that wasn't a yes or no. "What's in the bag?" she asked instead.

"Gabbs suggested I bring something along. You know how it is for us islanders. We never visit a house empty-handed."

It was true. "Gabbs?"

"My daughter, she's sixteen," Spencer said, smiling affectionately.

Della felt a sharp piercing stab in her heart. "That's nice," she struggled to say, feeling a hard lump in her throat. "Any other children?"

Spencer reached into his bag and started pulling out plastic containers and lining them up. "Nicole, she's my eldest, and Jesse. Three girls who are equally the love and bane of my life," he joked.

29

"Here you go, omelets, bacon, pancakes and hash browns. An American breakfast, only second best to our callaloo and boiled banana. I didn't know where to go for our food up here."

He rummaged through the other bag. "Can't have pancakes without Aunty's syrup and squirty cream," he declared with a toothy grin.

Della took out two plates and started sharing, giving him her share of the bacon.

"I'm not married," Spencer offered suddenly, just in case her imagination was running off in the wrong direction.

"How come?"

"My wife died when Gabbs was seven."

"I'm sorry."

"Don't be. It was a long time ago," he replied, shrugging. There had been plenty of women after his wife.

"Did I know her?"

"I met Tanya at university here. She came from Barbados."

For some reason, Della thought his children would be white, but then silently scolded herself. After all, he was a white Jamaican, and his wife could have been a white Bajan. Why these thoughts had suddenly taken over her mind, she didn't know. And if they mattered, she didn't even try to understand.

"Reach up there and get the tray down for me please," she said to Spencer.

Spencer reached on top of the cupboard and felt for the tray. Pulling it down, he smiled. Similar trays could be found in homes all over Jamaica. It was a black wicker tray with the lignum vitae and the hummingbird in one corner. Ackee, Jamaica's national fruit, and the Coat of Arms in the other. The images were surrounded by the words Out of Many One People, the national motto.

She indicated for him to go into the living-room and turned down the TV. Mr. Motive refused to move so Della scooped him up and put him gently on the floor. He meowed in protest and stopped to glare at them both before walking out of the room.

"Tell me what you've been doing all these years, Della," said

30

Spencer, as they started to eat.

"Not much to tell really," Della said with a self conscious shrug. She suddenly felt jaded, old and fat.

"Come on. You used to have all these dreams and plans," Spencer urged. "Remember we used to lie under the tamarind tree in your yard and plan our lives?" He smiled at the memory. "You said you were going to marry me."

She gasped in protest. "I was six years old!"

"I was always a part of your plans, Della," he noted with a tinge of sadness. "And when you were older you said you were going to become a doctor, and I'd never have to live with my mean father again. You promised to take care of me forever and ever."

Della vividly remembered that conversation. Spencer had just got a beating and had welts on his legs thanks to the switch his father had used. He'd come to her crying. She remembered wiping away his tears and giving him a slice of her mango.

She'd believed their love would have lasted forever too.

"Some pipe dreams I had going there huh, Spencer," she laughed shakily.

They were silent for a while before Spencer finally asked, "What happened, Della?"

"You passed me over for some red skin gyal."

"I did not!"

"You did. The night of your party. I saw you!"

"Doing what?"

"Having sex," Della said angrily. "Under our tree!" The tamarind tree was their special place.

Spencer had the decency to look embarrassed. "I was not having sex, I was just fooling around."

"And that makes it okay?"

"I was eighteen. I had too much to drink, and you'd been giving me the cold shoulder all week!"

"And that gave you the right to take up with another woman in front of our friends! You were so selfish, Spencer."

His birthday party had been a well-attended affair. The cream of

Jamaican society were out in full sparkling glory.

The Chandler-Wrights lived to impress and they'd gone all out to make sure their younger son had the time of his life and that their guests would talk about the party for years to come.

The entire grounds had been decorated with pepper lights. A four-man mento band played on the front lawns for the older guests, while a disco sound with huge speakers blared popular music around the back near the pool. Della remembered excusing herself to freshen up once Spencer had cut his birthday cake. She'd bumped into Mrs. Chandler-Wright, who usually talked to her out of necessity. Della was more than happy to do an errand she requested, but by the time she got back to the party Spencer had left.

It was Jeremy who later suggested they go look for him, and it was Jeremy who'd pointed to Spencer caught in a tight embrace with a girl under the tree.

Humiliated, as people stared at her pitifully, Della remembered walking away from the scene with Jeremy to the pool-house.

"I didn't sleep with her," said Spencer, bringing Della back to the present. "But I did see Jeremy leave your pool-house pulling up his zipper! He'd laughed when he saw me!"

Della scrambled off the sofa and went into the kitchen, slamming the tray on the counter. This argument was twenty years overdue.

"You slept with my brother!" Spencer roared, pinning her against the counter with a glare. "How could you do that to me?"

Tears welled up in Della's eyes and she wiped them away.

"But I didn't. I was just fooling around," she said, defending herself. She'd almost had sex with Jeremy, and the only reason she didn't was that he'd ejaculated all over her dress and then shouted at her for turning him on too fast. She'd rubbed herself raw in the shower, trying to get the smell of him off her skin. Jeremy had taken advantage of her distress that night, and she later realised she'd been set up by Spencer's family.

"With anyone but him, Della," Spencer breathed shakily, recalling the sting of the betrayal. "You hated him. You knew he was jealous of us. Do you know how I felt?" He pulled her hands away from her face and held them tightly in one of his.

"He rubbed my nose in it every chance he got until one day I'd had enough and broke his nose for him instead. We didn't talk for two years after that."

"I wasn't myself, Spencer," she cried. "I'd just seen you with another girl, your hand up her shirt! I felt sick to my stomach and I wanted to hurt you. But it turned out okay for you in the end, didn't it?" She sniffed through her tears and tried to smile. "You got married. Had your daughters."

"I wanted you to have my children, Della." Spencer's eyes filled with tears he didn't bother to hide.

"I'm sorry," she whispered.

He let her go and rubbed his hands over his face and turned away. She saw his shoulders lift and sag as he tried to control his emotions. It was all too much.

Della stepped forward and wrapped her arms around his broad back and hugged him close. This was Spencer, her first love. They were both hurting.

Spencer froze. This was the woman he would have laid down his life for. She was the one he'd planned to spend his whole life cherishing. How had it gone so wrong so fast for them? One minute they were happy and in love, her father encouraging them to get married every chance he got. And then she was gone. Just like that. Her parents had moved out, and it was almost a year before they came back and refused to talk to him and his family. They'd even replaced the fence with a brick wall so high you could only see their roof.

Spencer turned and rested his chin on Della's head and pulled her closer. Her scent reminded him of the freedom of the sea breeze.

After a moment she lifted her head to look at him. Spencer had never seen a look of such pure and open vulnerability in his life. They'd hurt each other so much, the only thing left was for them to start over.

He dipped his head and kissed her. A tentative brushing of lips, as he remembered their first kiss and a trust that was once whole.

33

Della's mouth trembled as it opened. Spencer groaned as her tongue flicked out to touch his. They allowed the kiss to linger, before Della finally took his hand and led the way to the bedroom.

Spencer watched her sleep. He'd spent hours loving her, remembering those places on her body that could make her giggle when he moved his hands a certain way. He didn't hesitate to reacquaint himself with those places that made her gasp or sigh into his mouth. Their loving had always been an experience, and perhaps that had been the problem. They'd been kids, too young to handle or appreciate such intensity, he thought as he moved one of her dreadlocks back over her shoulder.

He still couldn't get over the changes in her. She was tired and had smudges under her eyes, even in sleep she looked fatigued. There was something going on with her but he couldn't put a finger on it. There was a time when he felt like he knew her inside and out.

Della had been brought up to be a strict Christian. Her father was a well-known pastor, her mother a wealthy businesswoman and politician. They'd had big plans for her and Della didn't disappoint. She was an ace student, the class valedictorian, popular and rich. You simply had to like her. A lot of their friends didn't get their relationship, but it had always been Spencer and Della.

What the hell happened to her? When did she become a Rastafarian? She hadn't eaten the bacon this morning, Spencer noticed. Why was she working in a call centre in England when her quality of life would be so much better in Jamaica? It just didn't make any sense.

Hearing the melodious tones of Peter Tosh's *Johnny Be Good* on his BlackBerry, Spencer knew Gabbs was trying to reach him. He tried to slowly unwind himself from Della's smooth limbs, but she opened her eyes drowsily.

"Sorry, my phone is ringing." He kissed her nose and walked naked down the narrow stairs and spoke to Gabbs, who just wanted to know if breakfast had been a hit or not.

There was a mischievous smile on his face when he re-entered the bedroom and slipped into bed.

"I missed you, you know," he confessed, making himself comfortable.

"I'd missed you, too. But let's not talk about anything that will make us think too hard."

"I hope I didn't hurt you," he said, adjusting her head on his shoulder. "You were very tight. Almost as tight as the first time we made love. Remember that time?"

She smiled and swirled her finger around his nipple. It puckered. He'd always had sensitive nipples.

"My parents had gone to a church convention and we had the house to ourselves." She'd just turned sixteen, Della also recalled. "You'd come over the moment their car was out of sight." They both chuckled at the memory of him leaping over the fence.

"We'd gotten so hot and heavy, I was a walking hard-on for weeks."

"You made it very special."

He squeezed her. "It was. But you didn't answer my question. Did I hurt you just now?"

"No. I'm a little tender, but that's all. It's been a while," Della admitted shyly.

Della had always been his. He just couldn't picture her nor did he want to picture her having sex with another man.

"I know I don't have the right to ask, but how many men have there been since me?"

"There's only ever been you, Spencer," she whispered, burying her face into his strong neck. She felt his heart skip a beat at her revelation.

"Really?" He moved so that he could see her face. She looked everywhere but at him, and he gently grasped her chin, turning her to face him. "Really?" he repeated, watching as the blush crept up her neck. He'd never felt so humbled in his life. She was his. She'd always been his.

Spencer got up and went into the bathroom. Della could hear water running. He returned with a flannel.

"Let me do this for you," he offered with a gentleness that almost floored her. Tenderly, he bathed her with the cool cloth.

## CHAPTER FIVE

"What have you been doing all these years, Spencer?" Della asked later that evening.

Spencer, knowing Della would need to pace herself and recover from the little sleep over the past four nights, spent the afternoon with Gabbs. They'd gone to Broadmarsh, where instead of shopping they went exploring in the sandstone caves that ran beneath the historic city. For Spencer, it was humbling to see firsthand the poverty of Drury Street.

It was late evening before Spencer returned to Della's house. She cooked them a simple vegetarian dish. He washed the dishes, she dried and put them away. They were now lazing on the sofa, the murmur of the TV in the background, their legs intertwined as they relaxed like the in-sync couple they should have been years ago.

"As you know, my parents had bought that apartment for me off Hope Road, so I lived there for a while and worked at the department store down on King Street."

"You always said you would never work for your family."

"I did, but I was kind of lost for a while after you'd gone." Spencer looked at her pointedly and she lowered her head in discomfort.

"How did your wife die?" Della didn't want to be curious about the woman Spencer had married, but she couldn't help it.

"Brain aneurysm. She'd just dropped the girls off at school and, complaining of a headache, went to lie down. She didn't wake up."

"I'm so sorry. It must have been very difficult for you all."

"It was for a while, but we coped. Being the sole parent to three little girls kept me going." Spencer shrugged it off, but Della knew that it couldn't have been easy for him.

"How about you? I know you don't want to talk about it but what have you been doing all these years?" Spencer asked.

Della took a deep breath. "You know I was about to go and live on campus, don't you?"

"Yeah. It was all you would talk about," Spencer replied. Della sensed a tinge of bitterness in his tone.

"I was pregnant," she revealed, looking at the floor.

"Pregnant?" Spencer repeated blankly. When she'd gone missing, he'd thought about a possible pregnancy but simply dismissed the idea. Della would have told him. "Why didn't you tell me?" he asked softly.

"I was going to after your party," she said. "But then it all went wrong. We'd stopped talking, and I didn't know what to do."

"What did you do?" Spencer knew that an unplanned pregnancy in those days would have caused a serious scandal. But they'd have been okay. Everyone knew they were a couple. They would have gotten married a little sooner. That's all.

"Please don't judge me," Della begged, whispering.

"I won't," he promised. "You know I won't."

"My mother told me to have an abortion, saying as a politician she couldn't have a daughter with a baby and Daddy supported her. It would ruin all our lives, they said. Yours included." Her voice was flat and emotionless, as she remembered the time. The arguments. The ultimatums. The threats.

Spencer reached for her hand and folded his fingers tenderly around hers.

"After the party I was shattered. I thought you'd slept with that girl and I went a little crazy I think." A tear rolled down Della's cheek, and he brushed it away with his thumb.

"I'm sorry." He planted a kiss on her temple.

"We were both young," Della said. "My parents told yours and..."

"My parents knew?"

Della nodded. "Between the four of them, they sent me away."

"So you aborted my child and came to England and lived happily ever after, Della? Is that it?" Spencer knew he was being unreasonable but the betrayal cut him deeply.

"I didn't have the abortion."

"What?"

"I didn't have the abortion. I couldn't do it." She turned to face him. "I was staying in one of your parents' houses in Spanish Town. I was almost three months pregnant by that time. They said you'd moved on and was happy."

"They lied," Spencer stated grimly. "Then what happened?"

"A doctor and nurse came to the house. They'd planned to do the abortion and tried to tie me down." Tears were now rolling down Della's cheeks. "But I fought them. I fought them so hard I started bleeding anyway."

She stopped for a moment, vividly recalling the horror of that day. The shiny hook-like instruments placed on the side of the bed. The strip of leather for her to bite down on and the dirty finger nails of the doctor.

"They left then and next thing I remember I was on a plane." She looked at Spencer through her tears, imploring him to understand. "But..."

"But?" Spencer was getting angrier by the minute.

"It was a few weeks later that I realised I was still pregnant." Della took a deep breath. "I had my boys."

"Boys?"

"Twins. They were premature. Jacob and Isaac."

Spencer couldn't breathe. He felt as though a thick wet blanket had been thrown over his head.

"Jacob died three days later. Isaac struggled for a while, but he got better."

"Where is he now?"

"He lives not far from here."

Spencer got up with one swift movement. "Let's go."

Della gasped and looked at the clock. "We can't. It's the wrong time."

"It's still early. I want to meet my son. Now, Della!"

"I'm sorry, but you don't understand."

"What's not to understand? I have a son! My entire family lied to me. You kept him from me. What's not to understand!"

"I did what was best for everyone!" Della fired back.

"Really?" Spencer drawled, standing over her, his eyes ablaze with fury. She'd never seen him so angry. "You did what was best for you!"

"That's not true."

"Isn't it? You kept him from me to punish me. I kissed another girl, so what. I was eighteen. At eighteen we're allowed to do stupid things. It's fucking expected!"

She gasped at his viciousness but wasn't intimidated.

"Oh yeah. I was seventeen, pregnant and confused. You weren't there for me!"

"I wasn't allowed to be!"

There was a loud thumping on the living-room wall. "What the hell is that?" Spencer asked.

"My neighbours," said Della. "You're being too loud."

Spencer couldn't believe what he was hearing, and banged on the adjoining wall several times with all his strength.

"Feel better now?" Della asked sarcastically.

"Don't mock me, Della, or so help me God," he warned, trying to calm down. "You call him Isaac?"

"Isaac Adam Willett."

"At least you gave him some of my name." Spotting her handbag on the floor beside the sofa, he went to pick it up. "Come on."

"We can't go now. It's the wrong time!" Della exclaimed. She knew he didn't understand when she saw the confused look on his face. "Isaac has dyspraxia."

Spencer made the universal gesture of what-the-hell-is-that with his hands.

"It's sort of like Aspergers, ADHD and dyslexia rolled into one," she explained. "I need to stick to his routine or he'll be out of sorts."

"When can I meet him?" Spencer asked impatiently.

"I'll be going to see him at home in the morning."

"What time? I'll pick you up."

"No, you can't. He doesn't like strangers. I'll have to prepare him."

Spencer raked a hand through his hair. "You made us strangers, Della," he shot back, rubbing his hands over his face. "Fine. When?"

"Next week."

"I'll be in London next week."

Della shrugged.

"Does he know about me?"

"Yes."

"Thank you for that at least," Spencer said dryly, as he flung himself onto the sofa. Closing his eyes, he tried to come to terms with having a son. An adult son at that. "Tell me about him."

Della told him about her struggles as a single mother, raising a son who was considered difficult. She told him about the racism they endured in London and her decision to move up North, where the cost of living was cheaper. She talked about the small but strong Caribbean community that supported them.

"Why didn't you contact me, Della?" Spencer wanted to know.

"What was the point? Your parents wanted nothing to do with me, and my parents wanted me to give up Isaac for adoption. When I refused, neither one of us existed to them anymore, and it was easier and less painful for me to stay away."

"Easier for who? What about me?" Spencer asked. "I would have been there for you, you know that." His voice was thick with emotion.

"Here." Della offered him the photograph of Isaac she carried in her purse.

Spencer took it from her and scrutinized it, drinking in the features

41

of a young man who looked strikingly like his daughters. Without another word, he got up and headed for the front door.

\*\*\*

Blurry-eyed, Della yanked open the door expecting to see Spencer. To her surprise, she came face to face with a mixed-raced girl in black ankle boots, black leggings and a thick green jacket looking at her with a hostile expression on her pretty face.

"I'm Gabbriella Chandler-Wright, and I want to know what you've done to my dad," the young woman said.

Della wanted to laugh, but it was three in the morning and Gabbriella was obviously on her own. "How did you get here, and where is Spencer?"

"Dad got absolutely bladdered and I put him to bed," Gabbriella seethed. "Then I called a taxi."

"You'd better come in."

The young girl walked straight in, wiped her feet, looked at the carpet but walked on it anyway. Della recognised the stubborn angle of her chin as it was so like Isaac's.

In the light of the living room Gabbriella stared wide-eyed at Della. "What the hell, you're Della Willett?"

"Fraid so." Della looked down at the old but comfy blue chenille robe she was wearing. She'd just spent the last hour shaving every part of her body that hadn't seen a razor in years and concocted a cornmeal and coconut oil paste to make a body scrub. She felt beautiful.

"My dad's girlfriends are well peng, leggy and at least have hair extensions. You have dreadlocks!" Gabbriella pointed out, obviously scandalised.

'Peng' meant pretty, Della knew. Felicity had translated it for her the other night. She should have been upset by the comparison, but she'd been hearing remarks like that ever since she and the Spencer Chandler-Wright had become more than friends. She'd always been the one lacking, from her complexion to her religion and everything in between.

"This is it," said Della, gathering her locks in one hand and bringing them around to lie heavily against her chest.

"Wow. A Rasta," Gabbriella murmured, not bothering to hide her disappointment. "Well, anyway, Dad came home, I mean back to the hotel in a right state. He was down in the hotel bar for hours before they brought him up."

"Is he all right?"

"No thanks to you."

Gabbriella stared at Della as though she was something foul on her designer boots.

Della sighed deeply. She was wide awake now, emotionally drained and hungry. Spencer's daughter was a spitfire ready to do battle for her Dad. Gabbriella, Della thought, needed to know they were on the same side.

"I would never hurt him Gabbriella," she said softly. "What did he tell you?"

"All of it."

"All of it?"

"Well, most of it was drunken rambling," she revealed, "but I have a brother called Isaac who's twenty, and you never told Dad you were pregnant."

"There's a lot more to it than that," Della replied.

"Dad said Nanny and Granddad lied to him and kept you both apart."

Della nodded. "Would you like a hot chocolate?"

It was evident Gabbriella had not been expecting any niceties from her. "Yes please," she answered grudgingly.

"Take your jacket off," Della said, going into the kitchen. "And mind the cat."

Gabbriella was about to throw her jacket on top of the ball of fur. "You have a cat?"

"Mr. Motive. He's on the chair."

Gabbriella laughed. Mr. Motive was almost completely camouflaged lying on a grey throw with only his white paws giving him away. "That's so cute," she said, reaching for her mobile to take a picture. "That's for my Instagram."

"What's that?" Della asked.

"It's sort of like a blog, but with pictures. I'm aiming for 5,000 followers by New Year's," Gabbs said proudly, leaning against the door-jam to look at Della, who was grating nutmeg into the steaming mugs. "So you and my dad were a couple?"

"We were," Della answered, handing Gabbriella her mug. "Does Spencer know you're here?"

"God no. He'd kill me, and I'm already on punishment as it is."

"You'd better phone or send him a text to let him know you're with me." Della watched as Gabbriella pulled out a BlackBerry.

"Dad doesn't know about this one," she grinned, waving the phone and tucking it away. She quickly typed a text.

"How did you know where to find me?"

"You mean here? Easy. Dad is rubbish at directions, and he's got this map thingy on his phone. I just needed to look you up." She shrugged her narrow shoulders.

"He was always rubbish at directions" Della confirmed affectionately as they sat down and she told her about the time when they were fourteen and he'd got them lost in Hope Gardens.

"So I have a brother then, eh?" Gabbriella couldn't hide her eagerness to learn more about Isaac, and Della was touched by her concern.

"Yes, you do. Stay there." With that, Della went upstairs, rummaged around and brought down a box of photos and artwork. "This is Isaac's time capsule. I'll show you."

Nearly an hour later, Della and Gabbriella were still on the floor looking through pictures. Gabbriella asked lots of questions and even more when Della explained Isaac's dyspraxia. Gabbriella informed her that the star of the Harry Potter movies also had a mild form of the condition.

"You know, Della?" Gabbriella said sometime later.

"What's that, sugar?"

"You're all right."

"Thanks," Della smiled. "You're all right, too."

"You can call me Gabbs."

Della grinned. "C'mon. Let's get you back to the hotel. I'll call a taxi."

"You don't drive?" Gabbriella looked horrified.

"I used to. In fact I got my license the first time. I'm sure it took your Dad three or four tries though," she said with a twinkle in her eye. "But I don't have a car."

Gabbriella looked at her as though she had two heads.

"C'mon."

They were so busy talking and laughing that neither of them noticed Spencer until the door to the suite was closed behind them. He was just standing there, his hair all mussed, his chest bare, and his hands resting above the waist-band of his jeans.

"Where the hell have you been?" he yelled at Gabbriella. "I was just going to go look for you!" Spencer was beside himself with worry when he woke up and found the suite empty. He knew how impulsive Gabbs could be and pictured her tottering about the city in high heels, passing herself off as eighteen and hopping from club to club. "And what the hell are you doing with my daughter?" he shouted at Della.

"Eating her for supper," Della shot back. "What do you think I'm doing with her?"

Spencer tried to keep from smiling. Della always had a smart mouth.

"She got you there, Dad," Gabbriella chimed in, but then ducked her head quickly, as she knew what was coming when her dad looked at her with a raised brow and crossed his arms over his chest and waited. And waited some more. "Oh all right," she said, finally caving in with a dramatic sigh. She handed Spencer her BlackBerry then threw a sly wink at Della before going to her room.

"She came to my house ready to right the wrong she believed I did to you," explained Della.

"How."

"Something about looking in your phone for my address. She at least took a taxi and sent you a text. You had passed out apparently."

A tide of red touched his cheeks. "I fell asleep," he replied defensively.

"Humph."

"Thanks for bringing her home."

"Well, I wasn't about to let her leave by herself, was I? I'd better go."

Spencer gazed at her. She looked fresh, soft and loveable, and he felt the urge to wrap her in his arms again.

"Stay."

"Like a dog?" Della quipped.

He smiled. "Stay, because I need you to." He held out his hand and breathed a sigh of relief when she took it.

## CHAPTER SIX

Awakened by the beep of her mobile, Della reached for the device on the floor beside her clothes. She smiled when she saw that Isaac had sent her a text message of a smiley face and a thumbs up. That was his way of telling her he was up and expecting her later that morning.

"Where do you think you're going?" Spencer mumbled beside her, tightening his arm around her waist when she tried to wriggle to the edge of the bed.

"I've got to go."

He opened one eye to look at her. "What time is it? We've only just got to bed."

"It's half eight."

"I'm on holiday. I'm not supposed to see half eight," Spencer complained, pulling her even closer.

"I need to go," Della said, kissing his prickly chin. "I've got some errands to do, and I need to see Isaac."

He raised his head, looking at her quizzically.

"I know you want to meet him, but I've got to let him know you're here first. Isaac doesn't do surprises very well," Della explained, knowing Isaac could throw an almighty strop if his routine was interrupted in any way. And she knew she'd have to mention Spencer and Gabbs into their conversations several times before he really understood the significance of meeting his family.

Spencer wasn't happy, but he was willing to wait to learn more about his son's disability.

"Okay." He kissed her shoulder and moved his arm.

She turned to look at him pointedly as she bungled the white sheet around her naked body.

"What?" he asked.

"Turn round." She made a spinning gesture with her finger.

"You're kidding me, right?"

"No. Turn around."

"I've just spent the last hour or so kissing every inch of you, and you're shy?"

"It was dark, and besides, you've not seen this body since it was a teenager. A lot has changed since then."

"So I noticed," he chuckled.

Della's face flamed. "I know I'm fat Spencer but..."

"Not fat, Della. Nicely rounded and soft. I like it."

"You're just saying that because you don't want to hurt my feelings."

"If I wanted to hurt your feelings I would. But I am man enough to say that I appreciate you going to so much trouble to get rid of that forest I'd encountered earlier today," he said, grinning.

Della gasped. "You didn't just say that."

"But I do love the fact you went out and got all tidied up for me."

"Sorry to burst your bubble, but my spa was my bathroom."

"Seriously?"

"I prefer to use natural products on my skin." Della held out her arm to him. "Feel."

He did, running his hands along her smooth skin. "Next time my daughters say they want a spa day I'll be sending them to you."

"I still need you to close your eyes."

"Oh, for god's sake, woman," Spencer puffed, closing his eyes.

48

"You sound like Gabbriella," Della replied, wiggling from the sheets and reaching for her knickers and bra, quickly putting them on. "She's a great kid."

Spencer smiled. "She is."

"I showed her some photographs of Isaac."

"You told her about him?" Spencer asked, opening his eyes, hauling himself up and squashing a pillow behind his shoulders.

"No, you did."

"I didn't."

"She mentioned something about your drunken rambling, and she was curious."

Della watched fascinated as a tinge of red crept up his neck. "She's looking forward to meeting him. When are you going back to London?"

"Sunday evening or Monday morning. It depends on you, really."

"I'll sort something out for Sunday," Della promised.

"That's two days away."

"Patience never was one of your strong points. Was it, Spencer?"

He smiled and looked down to where the sheet had tented, showing his hard-on. "No, but that is."

She kissed her teeth and stepped beyond his reach when he grabbed after her. "I've got to go, and besides, I really don't want Gabbriella to see me here."

"She won't mind."

"She'll mind very much, as I'm not the usual type of women you bring home," Della pointed out. "It was almost like I'd committed a criminal offence being a Rasta!"

Spencer chuckled. "I'm very discreet. None of my daughters have even met, much less seen, any of my women. Since when did you go for the whole Rastafarianism thing, anyway?"

"Drop the ism," said Della.

"What?"

"It isn't Rastafarianism. I'm a Rasta and practise Rastafarian beliefs."

"There's a difference?"

"You're a Jamaican, Spencer. You're supposed to know it's not a religion."

"Never really thought about it to be honest. Does this mean you'll start selling brooms on the street and heading off to Africa?" he joked.

"The Bobo Shanti are strict Rastafarians who prefer to live independently in Bull Bay. Selling brooms is simply a way of supporting their community, Spencer," said Della, pressing her lips tightly together. She'd encountered this kind of ignorance before and was disappointed Spencer could display such lack of knowledge. Especially being a Jamaican.

"I'm sorry. I didn't mean to be judgemental," he apologised. "I know very little about the movement."

"If I was a Bobo Shanti, Spencer, I wouldn't be here, half naked with a man who was not my Kingman." She qualified, roughly grabbing a handful of her hair, twisting it and tying it loosely into a bun at her nape. "I'm very modern in my beliefs, and they are personal to me." She finished getting dressed in tense silence.

Spencer could see he needed to lighten the mood. He didn't want her to leave feeling the way she did.

"I've had many women since my wife died, Della, but you're my first real Rasta." He grinned.

Della gasped at the lascivious way he was looking at her. He made her feel as though she were a novelty toy to play with until a brighter one came along. She didn't feel special. She felt like one of many. Why did she jump into bed with him? They may have a history, but they really didn't know each other.

"Are you seeing anyone now?"

"Woman, I practically fell on you the moment I saw you. You think that is the action of a man having regular sex?"

"Thank you very much, Spencer. Nice to know I'm easy enough for you to relive your sexual frustrations on!"

"Don't be bloody stupid, and stop trying to start an argument because you think I hurt your feelings." With that Spencer jumped out of the bed and stood naked in front of her, the tip of his erection nudging her tummy. He cupped her face with his big hands and kissed her. "You are beautiful. I like the dreads and keep thinking of ways I can tie you up with your own hair. You're not fat. You're just right, and I love the way you made an effort to please me. But you'll need to educate me." He kissed her again. "Now get going before I tumble you into bed again." He kissed her nose before letting her go to pull on his jeans. "Now stop sulking. Where did you park your car?"

"Women my age don't sulk. We suppress the words we really want to say until we know you can handle it!" replied Della.

"Oh really?" Spencer challenged, pulling a thin blue jumper over his head before grabbing her by the waist. "Argument, sex or car?" He moved a hand down her thigh and lifting her leg so she could feel the promise of his erection.

"I don't have a car," she whispered, pressing her hips into him. She almost stumbled when he let her go.

"How can you not have a car? No, don't answer that. I'll get my keys."

"I'll call a taxi. You stay. I don't want Gabbriella to be alone in the suite."

She could see the indecision on his handsome face. "This is my city, Spencer. If I had my trainers I'd walk it back."

"I don't bloody well think so."

"Look at you sounding all British," Della teased. She reached for her phone and called a taxi. "What are you doing today?"

"Not sure yet. I'll leave it up to Gabbs," said Spencer.

"Well, you're within walking distance of the castle, and I think they've got some sort of art exhibition going on. So that should be nice," she advised.

"We can go to dinner later."

"Yes."

"What does Isaac like?"

Della smiled. "Ask Gabbriella. We spent the whole night talking about him. I'm sure she'll love knowing that she knows more about her brother than you do. Let her have her moment."

"You really understand girls, don't you?"

"You forget I'm one?" Della teased, as they walked through the suite.

"Oh, I'd never forget," Spencer replied, pressing his erection against her bottom and moving to skim her nipples with his fingers.

"Bye," Della whispered a few moments later when he had just about reduced her to a puddle at his feet.

With a knowing smile, Spencer opened the door. "Seeyainabit," he teased with a wink.

## CHAPTER SEVEN

It was late Sunday night and the city was buzzing, even though the temperature had dropped dramatically. The air was frigid. Della was dressed in a long black dress with a deep neckline that stretched across her breasts and sleeves that reminded Spencer of a wizard's robe. Her hair was styled in a complicated bun with several ropey strands trailing down her narrow back. He'd never seen her look so pretty, young and carefree. She was even wearing lipstick the exact shade of red as the scarf around her neck.

"This way," Della urged as they approached a club that looked like many of the others they'd past as she had insisted they walk from his hotel. The clubs frontage was a blaze of green and yellow lighting with a wooden cut-out of a zebra running from a snarling lion. Two heavy-set bouncers—one white, one black—manned the door to the lobby. Spotting them approaching, they opened the doors, smiled at Della as she walked past but gave Spencer a sharp once-over which sent his hackles rising.

Meanwhile, Gabbriella was back at the hotel sulking because she'd wanted to join them, but Spencer had quickly vetoed the idea. He knew Della had raised Isaac as best as she could. She was a single parent, raised the boy with little money, on benefits and living in a council house. But Spencer had already decided that Gabbriella wasn't going anywhere near her brother until he had checked him out. He didn't consider himself a snob, but he had his standards.

He followed Della into the dimly lit club and immediately looked at the stage, seeing four men. A couple of them had on sunglasses, and two had long beards, but they all sported dreadlocks of various lengths and wore rasta coloured scarves over their shoulders. Tacky leather medallions finished off their look. How trite, Spencer thought. He froze when he saw a younger version of himself playing the drums at the back of the stage.

He didn't know what he'd actually been expecting but this? His son was a Rastafarian? He should have expected it what with Della being what she was. But to see his son a Chandler-Wright with his hair matted together and even from this far Spencer could see that his eyes were bloodshot. The boy was high and so completely involved with the music that he didn't bother to wipe the sweat from his forehead. Spencer was vaguely aware of the band playing a rendition of *Ghost Town* by The Specials.

He must have stopped walking, as he felt the soft pull of Della's hand on his wrist as she meandered them across the small crowded room. His shoes were making sticky tape noises as they crossed the floor. It was the kind of place where if you wanted to dance you had to do it sitting down. There wasn't enough room to sway.

He watched as Isaac tapped his sticks, counting down the beat as the lead singer went into another Ska song from the early eighties that Spencer dimly remembered.

"Okay?" Della asked him. It wasn't unusual for her to watch Isaac play, and she was glad she'd changed their plans and had Spencer meet his son at the club. Isaac's mood was often lighter here and he was more receptive to visitors after a gig.

She signalled to the bartender and put up two fingers when he held up a bottle of her favourite cranberry juice. She nodded again when he indicated ice.

Inside the Zulu bar resembled a template of the Motherland.

Shadowy shapes of African countries, traditional water jugs and spears adorned the red walls. Everything about the place felt false and corny. The wooden pew-like benches were hard, and Della knew you had to get there very early to get one of the few cushions that were scattered around. But the atmosphere was always good, and there was never any trouble with the patrons who came more for the live music than for the cheap alcopops and beer on offer.

Della sat back and made herself as comfortable as she could. Ras Kevin was belting away in a gravelly voice that was as perfectly suited to reggae as it was to rock. Along with Isaac, the band's two bass players were the original members who joined him just over two years ago. Ras Dread, the newest and youngest member at just nineteen, played the keyboard.

Della couldn't help noticing how closely Spencer was watching Isaac. He was leaning slightly forward on the bench, his shoulders tense and his eyes narrow as he stared without giving anything away, totally focussed on the stage. Della couldn't judge his mood. He'd gone from playful father with Gabbriella this morning to ardent lover with her when he'd taken her home to get dressed this evening, to being suspicious and remote as they'd walked into town. She didn't know him like this, and she pushed the niggly thought that she didn't know him as an adult firmly from her mind. He'd once been her best friend. She trusted him.

Just then, Isaac caught her eye and winked and she winked back. A girl in the seat in front thought the gesture was for her and went into a fit of girlish giggles with her friend.

Della shook her head. Tonight Isaac was wearing a red string vest that showed off his muscular shoulders and arms and a red, green and gold bandanna that kept his hair back. There was always a gaggle of girls gathered at the stage door, wanting his autograph after he played. Della knew how difficult it was for him to sign his name in that casual effortless manner. They'd practised together for hours to get his signature into an artistic but manageable scrawl.

Della gave thanks every day that her son had found his calling. He'd been able to channel his creativity into something positive, instead of sitting on the damn sofa playing games every day. The band gave him purpose, and even though he couldn't read sheet music, he had taught himself the drums and guitar and was now learning the saxophone. Isaac didn't talk a lot, but he had depth, loyalty and a quiet intelligence that surprised many. Della was literally bursting with pride as only she knew what it had taken for him to get to this point.

Then she saw him frown and miss one, two then three beats. His gaze darkened and his lips flattened into a tight line. The whole moment couldn't have lasted more than five seconds but the other musicians noticed and Della could see the lead ask him what was up. With a shake of his head, Isaac closed his eyes and effortlessly picked up the beat again.

Spencer didn't realise he'd been holding his breath until his lungs had started to burn and he let it out with a swoosh. His son was giving him a hostile stare. The only other time Spencer had felt this cold was the week he'd once spent in Toronto one winter. There was no love in the gaze that was levelled at him.

***

The band had left the stage and the club was emptying. Spencer sat sipping the red juice Della had pushed into his hands as they waited. He didn't know what he was feeling, but he knew he'd rather be drinking a shot of white overproof rum. Reggae music was playing from several speakers set high on the walls. One of the Marley boys' Spencer knew as Gabbs had gone through a phase of having the bloody song on repeat for weeks. The lighting was now bright enough for him to see how shabby the place really was with dust in the corners and shallow puddles of spilled drinks on the wooden floor that looked as though it hadn't been mopped in weeks.

"Just what did you tell the boy about me?" Spencer asked suddenly, turning to Della. Isaac had been downright hostile with that single look speaking volumes.

"The boy?" Della asked incredulously, quickly forgiving his

rudeness. He must be nervous. "I've always been honest with him."

"Honest how?" Spencer retorted with a growl.

"Just that you didn't know about him, until now," Della shrugged.

"That's it?"

"Just about," Della said. Spencer noted a guilty look in her eyes.

"What else?" he asked grimly, knowing he wasn't going to like her answer.

"He's always been curious about my life in Jamaica before he was born. So I told him."

Spencer laughed, an unpleasant sound as he threw back his head in exasperation barely noticing the galvanised air conditioning tunnels that criss-crossed the ceiling. "That's just great Della. Just great. So now he thinks I'm a rich bastard, with a family that wanted him dead because his mother wasn't good enough for us!"

"That's not it at all!" Della gasped, standing up with her hands on her hips. "I was honest enough to explain what happened and the circumst—"

Spencer glanced over Della's shoulder and stood up. Turning, Della saw Isaac behind her, and by his expression she knew he'd overheard their argument. Isaac didn't like arguments and avoided confrontations whenever possible. His dyspraxia made it difficult for him to express himself verbally, forcing him to lash out instead. Sometimes with his fists.

"Hey, you were great out there tonight," said Della, moving towards him. Isaac ignored her. He just took a single step forward and shifted so that she was behind him.

"Don't you ever shout at mi mother again, ya hear," Isaac snarled at Spencer.

Spencer pulled himself to his full height, which made him slightly taller than his son. Another time he would have admired the loyalty of the boy. But not right now.

"Spencer," Della quickly moved between the two men, placing a hand on each of their chests. "Isaac, he wasn't shouting. We were just talking."

For an awful moment Spencer thought the boy was going to get physical with him.

Della watched anxiously as Isaac took a few deep breaths, knowing he was mentally counting to sixteen like his support worker had taught him. Counting to ten had never worked for him. He eventually looked down at her and smiled.

Satisfied that he wasn't about to throw a punch at his father, Della turned to Spencer with an expectant look on her face and graciously moved away so the two men could at least shake hands. This wasn't how she'd envisioned their meeting, but the devil had a way of sticking his fork where one least expected it.

The two men shook hands.

"Isaac, this is your father," said Della. Isaac stepped backwards as quickly as he could. His whole stance was one of tight rejection.

"So now dis man turn up and we just what?" Isaac asked. Like his mother, Isaac regularly slipped into his Jamaican accent whenever the mood took him. Tonight it came out in every aggressive breath he took. "Not nobody talk to mi mother inna dat bloodclaat tone."

Della gasped. Isaac was always respectful around her and never swore. What was wrong with him? Hell, she thought, what was wrong with Spencer, standing there with his legs apart and his jaw shoved forward as though he was gunning for a fight! Della didn't understand. What was wrong with these men?

Two girls approached them then and asked Isaac for his autograph. Casting a dirty look at Spencer and an intense look at his mother, Isaac threw an arm around each girl, turned and walked off.

"Well, that went well," Spencer mocked a few seconds later as he watched them disappear out the front door.

"What do you expect?" Della replied, picking up her scarf and winding it with aggressive flicks around her neck. "You shouldn't have been shouting at me like that!"

"I was not shouting," Spencer said as he tracked her out onto the street. "Where are you going?" Della had turned right instead of left towards Maid Marion Way, where his hotel was located.

"Home," said Della.

"We need to talk about this."

"No. You ruined it tonight with that snobbish attitude anyone can smell a mile off! You stink with it!" she shouted, her eyes hot and accusing. "If you didn't want to meet him Spencer you could have just said so."

"What the hell is this? Of course I wanted to meet him. It —"

"Oh yeah? From the moment we stepped inside you were looking down your nose at the place." She threw at him and stomped off.

"So what? The place is a dump."

"But by whose standards? Yours?"

"That's not what I meant! And stop putting words in my mouth and jumping to conclusions. I just thought he'd be playing somewhere a little classier. That's all."

"What's really going on here, Spencer?" Della asked, walking back towards him.

The late late film had just finished at The Corner House cinema behind them and the place was now swarming with university students. Sensing a heated argument, several stopped to watch the exchange with open curiosity.

"I asked you a question?" Della went on, ignoring the crowd and circling him. She was vaguely aware of a large TV screen advertising the Christmas Pantomime across the street.

Spencer ran his hands through his hair in frustration. "The kid's a Rastafarian," he shouted, immediately regretting his outburst, especially when someone in the crowd booed him.

Della pulled herself up to her full diminutive height. "So am I," Della reminded him.

"I know that." Spencer took a step towards her but stopped when he noticed her moving backwards to the very edge of the pavement and inches from the busy road swarming with green taxis. "I just didn't think he'd be one, too."

They stared at each other for a long while. The look of disappointment in Della's eyes gutted him completely. Her shoulders sagged and her chin lowered as tears gathered in her dark eyes.

"I'm a Rastafarian as well, Spencer," she whispered again with a voice laced with bitterness.

"You're different. You don't go around referring to yourself as I and I and smoking weed. You made a choice. Isaac didn't have a choice."

"How do you know that? I raised my son to value himself and make his own choices. What he is today is who he wants to be. Living his life by the Livity is what he wanted to do. I had nothing to do with the choices he's made."

"Does he smoke weed?" Spencer hated himself for asking, but he wanted to know.

Della looked straight at him. "Not all Rastafarians smoke weed, Spencer. Not all Rastafarians have dreadlocks." The crowd starting clapping. "And for a man of such intellect I find your judgements prejudicial. I don't want you hurting my son with those sweeping generalisations!" The crowd cheered in agreement. "I'm going home now."

"Della—," Spencer pleaded, taking a step towards her.

"Don't." She stuck out her hand to stop him. "Let me go home."

Spencer watched as she disappeared into the crowd.

# CHAPTER EIGHT

A few days later, as he looked out at the London skyline from his sixth floor office, Spencer decided he had to fix things with Della. He walked to the small kitchenette in his office and made himself some strong black coffee. It was good, scorching hot, dark and bitter. Not that herbal stuff Della liked to give him.

He hadn't seen or spoken to Della since their argument Sunday night. First thing Monday morning, he'd taken Gabbriella by her place to say goodbye but she wasn't in, or had simply refused to open the door.

Spencer swivelled his chair to look out the window again, recalling the conversation he'd had with his daughter on the drive back.

"I don't see why I couldn't stay with Della until you came back," Gabbriella whined. "Della wouldn't have minded. She thinks I'm amazing."

"I don't know why?" Spencer muttered, feeling sharp needle-like pains radiating up from his shoulders and neck to finish in a knot of tension at his temples.

"That's not a nice thing to say to your daughter, Dad!" Gabbriella exclaimed. "I just wanted to stay. That's all."

"No. And as you so casually forgot to apply to any sixth forms and college courses, you'll best find yourself a job until enrolment in January," Spencer replied, feeling for his sunglasses in the pocket of the car door. He slipped them on with relief.

"I could find a job in Nottingham," said Gabbriella.

"For God's sake, Gabbriella! Five days ago you were bawling your eyes out because you were leaving London and your friends!" Spencer turned on the radio. "You're not staying in Nottingham, and that's final!"

"No, it's not," she retorted. "I didn't even get to meet Isaac!"

"And until I know him better, you won't be!"

She crossed her arms and turned to glare at him. "What did you do?" she asked, eyeing him suspiciously. "You always spoil things."

Spencer gripped the steering wheel harder, wishing he could let the car accelerate to it's full speed and rip up the motorway.

"I met him."

"And?"

"I didn't like what I saw."

"Why? What was he doing?"

"Playing drums in a vintage reggae band called The Steel Lions or something."

"How amazing is that. A drummer." Gabbriella took out her phone, plugged in the auxiliary cable, and the next thing Spencer heard was the voice of the band's lead singer belting out *El Shadaai*.

"Is that them? Is that an original song?" Gabbriella asked, bubbling with excitement.

"That's them. The original is by Jahmali, I think."

"Dad, sometimes you really freak me out with all this reggae music stuff," she told him admiringly. "Does he look like us? I know I saw a picture, but he was younger then."

"He looks like me, and I could see a bit of your sister in him."

"Nicole or Jesse?"

"Nicole."

"Nothing of me?"

"No, not you."

Gabbs went silent for a moment. From the corner of his eye, Spencer could see her biting her lip, deep in thought. It was never a good sign when his youngest daughter started putting her brain to work.

She turned down the radio's volume and turned as far as her seatbelt would allow to face her dad."A brother. What did you talk about? How tall is he? I can't wait to meet him."

Spencer could hear the enthusiasm in her voice. "You'll meet him when I know him better."

"Why. What's wrong with him?"

"And I don't want you around him until then."

"What the hell is wrong with you, Dad? He's your son and Della is just fab. I like her. You do like her. Don't you, Dad?" Gabbs asked worriedly. Instead of responding, Spencer let the silence linger.

"What the hell, Dad. I can't believe you have a problem with Della," she said. "She's amazing, and I noticed you didn't have a problem having sex with her." Gabbs finished tartly and folded her arms high on her chest.

"Gabbriella," Spencer growled. "Enough."

"No, you always spoil things. You made Nicole move out, just because you didn't like her boyfriend. Stay or go. What kind of a choice is that?" She was on full throttle now. "And Jesse left as soon as she finished school because she couldn't stand the thought of living with you and your stuffy rules any longer. And as soon as I get a job I'm gone!"

"Make sure you leave the key," said Spencer, trying to hide the pain her words had caused him. He'd heard it all before, just in different variations, depending on which daughter was shouting at him at the time.

"You have control issues, Dad, and I'm not talking to you anymore."

Those were the last words Gabbriella had spoken to him in three days. They'd come full circle, and it was back to the silent treatment again. She had left him with an uncomfortable feeling he wasn't ready to explore right now. He'd always been fair with his daughters, he tried to convince himself. Feeling a headache coming on, he reached into his bottom drawer for the bottle of pain-killers.

\*\*\*

"Fuck this shit. I'm going on my break," Fliss declared, tossing down her headset and getting up. It was one of the busiest nights they'd ever had. Multiple promotions were going out globally in the run-up to Christmas.

"Sit down, Felicity!" Monica-Louise ordered, storming over in a too-small skirt she should have given up when she was a size sixteen. "It's not your break time yet!"

"It is," Fliss objected, looking at the time on her mobile with blatant disregard for the floor's no-phone policy.

"Don't argue with me. You'll take your break when the calls die down."

Although she was on a call, Della watched the exchange closely, ready to intervene if she needed to. She liked Fliss and admired her fighting spirit, but she also knew Fliss was likely to sabotage her own life simply because she hadn't learned to control her mouth.

"Can I go to the loo?" Fliss asked sarcastically, breaking the ten-second stand-off.

Monica-Louise made a show of looking at her watch. "I'll put you on a disciplinary if you're not back here within five minutes. Wrap up that call, Ingrid," she said, as she walked past the blonde. "You've been warned about your call times."

It was a hectic night, with call after call coming in. It didn't help either that the floor captain kept shouting the number of calls that were in the queue. Double figures apparently.

Della had never seen their captain look so stressed. For her part, Della took things in her stride, opting to simply take one call at a time and not stress about it. Over the years, she'd learned to put things into their proper perspective. She was grateful for the money she earned and liked the hours and the people she worked with. But it was just a simple call-centre job hovering on the periphery of her life. Isaac was what really mattered.

She'd hoped Spencer was going to matter too, and it hurt her deeply to think of how he'd turned out. Just like the rest of his family.

Della felt used. Sleeping with a man she barely knew. It didn't matter that they used to be lovers. It didn't matter that they had even been friends. That was a long time ago and she should have remembered that instead of falling into bed with him. What was she thinking? She'd been guilty of holding onto a memory of her knight in shining armour, her happily ever after, her frog turned prince and all that other romantic malarkey. But not anymore, she decided. She'd been happy before Spencer came along, and she would be happy again. She didn't need him. She needed to remember that.

Her musing was interrupted by a long piercing sound that rang loudly throughout the building with a two second pause in between.

"What the hell is that?" Mackenzie shouted over the din.

"The fire alarm," Della announced, stifling a yawn. She'd only ever experienced one other fire drill in all the years she'd been working at the centre.

"All right everybody. This is not a drill," Monica-Louise exclaimed, palming her hands around her mouth to shout again. "This is not a drill. Outside now!" She chucked her bag over her shoulder and moved quickly towards her colleagues. "Ingrid, end that call now!"

Della grabbed her own bag and shoved the picture of Isaac and Mr. Motive inside it before dashing towards the stairs with the rest of the team.

It was a mess.

The night team had rarely practised the fire drill and never at this time of the morning. They were tired and although they moved, it was more like a zombie shuffle.

"The other stairs you lot!" Monica-Louise directed with exasperation as the team moved towards the normal stairwell. Some were even waiting for the lift!

Two lots of teams eventually converged at the other end of the floor waiting with near panic as Mackenzie and Jarrett tried to figure out the double metal doors.

"Here, let me." Lifting up the long handles Della got them open and stood aside as they all rushed passed.

"Be careful!" Monica-Louise shouted. "Does everyone know where the meeting point is?"

There was a general chorus of noes and yeses.

"My lot," she looked at her team. "We're across the street at Franco's. I'll be there in a sec. Della? Do a head count. We had a full quota of staff tonight," she advised quickly.

"Jarrett you wait with me." She told the young man as everyone else walked off in an excited chatter.

They crossed the empty street and stood opposite the front of their building looking for signs of a fire. The building was about seventy years old and looked it. Wide strips of aluminium framed large rectangular windows dressed with faded green panels. There were no other lights on other than the fluorescent lights from their floor.

"This is so exciting," Mackenzie declared going into the café. "Anyone for a coffee?"

They crowded inside and placed their orders.

"Is everyone accounted for?" Monica-Louise asked Della sometime later.

"Fliss isn't here." Della admitted reluctantly noticing the tinge of pink on the other woman's cheeks.

"Oh for goodness sake, that girl." The Floor Captain muttered just as two fire engines pulled up and she went to talk to the crew.

Della pulled out a chair at the table nearest to the half opened door so she could look out. It was bitterly cold outside and although she was wearing boots, a long skirt and her jumper she was freezing without her coat. None of them had their coats. Ingrid sat opposite her, wrapping her hands around her cup of tea trying to keep warm.

"You all right Ingrid?"

"I guess. I was taking a really big order when the alarm went off. I hope he'll call back."

"You're commission has been really something these past few months. What's your secret?" Della teased and watched curiously as her friend flushed and looked down. "Mr. Mcgrail was really concerned when the alarm went off." Ingrid revealed as though Della was supposed to know who Mr. Mcgrail was.

Della shrugged. Her customer had wanted her to finish the damn order! She didn't understand people sometimes. They could be so selfish and where was Fliss? She thought worriedly, looking across the street. There wasn't any flames or smoke bellowing out of the windows she noted with relief.

Ingrid's mobile rang just then and she looked at the screen and grinned. "Excuse me, I need to take this." She went outside.

As soon as Ingrid got up Priya sat down.


"Della?" Priya whispered, adjusting her black scarf and leaning forward.

"Yes chick?" Della used the pet name she'd given her.

"Do you think Fliss pulled the alarm?"

The question startled Della for a moment as it was so absurd.

"No, well I don't think so."

"She went to the toilet just before the alarm went off that's all."

"I don't think she'd do that Priya. But don't say anything." Della advised solemnly.

There was a shocking stillness in the air when the alarm stopped and they all looked outside watching as Monica-Louise and a fireman walked towards them. Fliss was trailing behind them with her head bent down low.

"Felicity was stuck in the lift," the Floor Captain announced spitefully. "This lovely fireman had to get her out."

Felicity pulled herself up to her full height and tried to laugh it off when the rest of the team started grilling her, but it was only Della who noticed how unusually red her eyes were.

"Well, we might as well have a meeting while we're all here," Monica-Louise said, collecting a cup of tea. "Right, well before all this," she continued, pointing to the building and the café with a dramatic sweep of her arms, "I was reading an email from the London office and they're going to launch a new incentive for the three night teams."

"Cool," Lucia said. "We never get anything."

"What type of incentive and what's the prize?" Della asked.

"Stats. From your call times, to your sales and general customer service," Monica explained. "Basically—"

"What's the prize?" Mackenzie cut in knowing how Monica-Louise could waffle on about their stats.

"We've never had it so big," Monica answered, smiling. "Seven nights at an exotic location."

"Ooh," everybody said in unison.

"Five nights in London." Monica waited for another round of oohs to finish. "And last but not least a weekend in a castle somewhere."

They booed.

"Who in their right mind would want to stay in some draughty castle when we can go to St Lucia?" asked Jarrett.

"Or Kathmandu, Thailand!" Mackenzie piped in, clapping with excitement.

"Kathmandu is in Nepal, you idiot," Lucia corrected rolling her eyes.

"Whatever," Mackenzie dismissed, flicking his slender wrist. "Kathmandu, Phuket. They're both fab this time of year! Just where is this exotic location anyway? For all we know Benidorm could be their equivalent of exotic!" he finished, bugging his eyes at them in horror

They all laughed.

"I don't know yet. But it starts for the month of December. So get selling, guys," Monica-Louise told them.

Another hour went by before they were let back into the building. The next set of shifts was due to start in thirty minutes. Clearly in a good mood, Monica-Louise let them leave early. Della decided to use the free time to drop in on Isaac and make breakfast. But when she knocked and let herself in, he wasn't there. His bike was missing. For a moment she wondered if he had gone back on his promise.

## CHAPTER NINE

"She's here."

"What? Who is this?"

"It's Della, and I'm ringing to tell you Gabbriella turned up this morning."

"Della?" Spencer lurched upright in his chair and gripped his mobile tighter. "I don't understand? I saw Gabbriella last night at dinner. What do you mean she's with you?"

"Look, I don't know what kind of relationship you have with your children. I'm not here to judge, but Gabbriella was waiting for me when I got off work this morning," she explained. "Do you want to talk to her?"

"Not yet," said Spencer, sensing the familiar pinpricks moving up and down his shoulders, making his eyes water. He rubbed his left temple, trying to ease the pain. "Is she all right?"

Miles away, Della looked at Gabbriella who was sat on the floor stroking Mr. Motive without a care in the world.

"She's fine."

"How did she get there?"

"Bus, apparently."

"Why?"

"Why did she take the bus? I'm not sure."

"No, I meant why is she there?" he asked. "I told her she needs to start looking for a job."

"Yes, well, you need to take that up with her."

There was silence for a moment as Spencer digested Gabbriella pulling such a stupid stunt and also the coolness in Della's voice. He'd been trying to get a hold of her for days. "Are you all right, Della?" Spencer asked quietly. She'd been back in his life less than a week but he missed her.

"Why wouldn't I be?" Della replied lightly. Too lightly he thought.

"Last time I saw you, you were walking away from me. Again."

"People have their views, Spencer," Della said, moving away from Gabbriella. "It's just a pity yours are so different from mine. It could have been so different."

"No, don't say that." Spencer closed his eyes and leaned back in his chair. "I'm sorry, okay?"

"Sorry for what exactly?"

"Of all the bloody—," he started, before Della cut him off.

"Look, I've just got in from work," she said. "I'm tired and I need to go to bed. I don't mind Gabbriella staying at all."

"I'll come get her tomorrow."

"No!"

"What?"

"She may as well stay until the weekend."

"If you're sure."

"Of course I'm sure."

"Will you be seeing Isaac?"

"Of course."

"Before the weekend?"

"I won't introduce them if you don't want me to, Spencer."

"It's not that. It's just that I'd rather be there, that's all."

"Humph. This is my house and if my son comes round to visit, I'll be letting him in as I always do. If Gabbriella is here, well..."

"I'd still rather—"

"Look!" Della interrupted, losing patience. She really was tired and in no mood for this. "I'm not having this conversation with you. Do you want to speak to her now?"

"Yes," Spencer replied quickly.

Della must have put her hand over the mouthpiece as they sounded as though they were having a conversation under water.

"Spencer?"

"It's okay. She doesn't want to talk to me. I get it."

"I'm sorry."

"Course you are. My daughter takes off to stay with a woman she barely knows just to piss me off!" he raged unreasonably.

"Right now, Spencer Chandler-Wright, I can see why she left. Ring us when you've found some compassion and not a minute before!"

The phone went dead, and Spencer fought the urge to hurl it across the room. Women! It was at times like this he wished he'd had sons then he immediately sobered as he remembered.

Walking back to his desk, he pulled out his iPad and did a YouTube search on The Steel Lions.

\*\*\*

"Here." Spencer thrust a soft grey teddy bear at Della, took a large step that brought him into her living room and swiftly caught her as she stumbled backwards. He'd woken her up. Good.

"Sorry about the time," he lied casually. "I wasn't sure about your sleeping pattern." He walked through to her kitchen and turned on the kettle.

He hadn't made it to Nottingham last week, thinking they needed some time apart. Gabbriella being here meant he still had access to Della and that's what he needed. Access to Della.

All this time Della hadn't said a single word and was just standing there barefooted in her blue robe, with one pocket hanging half off. Spencer noticed that her toes were painted red and her ankles looked slim and dainty. He'd never noticed her feet before and was surprised to feel the blood rush down to his groin.

Looking at her now with the soft sleepiness in her dark eyes and pillow creases down one side of her face, he was tempted to pick her up and take her straight back to bed. She probably sensed his intention, as she gave him a hard look and then cut her eyes after him. It had been a very long time since he'd seen that rude gesture and it made him chuckle.

With a sudden movement, he grabbed her, swept one hand down her back to plaster her small frame against his and buried his face in her neck. She smelt of vanilla, sleep and cotton sheets, and he loved it.

He trailed a row of small kisses up her neck but she wrenched herself away when he tried to capture her mouth.

"No," she said, clutching the bear in front of her.

"Why not?" Usually he'd have carried her up the stairs and already be deep inside her.

"Gabbriella."

"Where is she?" he asked, resigned to the fact he'd have to wait to take Della to bed.

"Not here."

Spencer smiled and moved towards Della again, but she stepped away.

"I'm going to get dressed," she announced and fled, his laughter trailing her as she raced up the stairs.

Spencer searched her cupboards but found nothing stronger than a packet of sorrel tea. He'd never had the traditional Christmas drink as a tea before. Following the instructions, he made himself a mug before returning to the living room.

He could see evidence of his daughter's presence everywhere. Three pairs of Converse lined up neatly under the table, the glossy weekly magazine she favoured lying on the floor beside the single chair and her purple jumper hanging on the back of the door. She'd made herself at home, he thought with a frown, taking a sip of the surprisingly good tea.

Upstairs, Della pulled on a pair of black leggings, black long sleeved t-shirt and her favourite dark green fleece with the zip and hood.

"Did you like the bear?" Spencer asked when she finally came downstairs. He knew they were going to fight but he wanted to delay it for as long as possible. Life with Della never used to be this fraught with tension, and Spencer longed to recapture the days of laughter and light, when he had been the centre of her life. Deep down he felt like a selfish bastard, but Della was his. She'd always been.

"I guess I'm not a soft toy type of person," offered Della.

She wasn't going to make this easy on him, he concluded, smiling silently to himself. "You didn't get it."

Della frowned and watched warily as Spencer drained whatever was in his cup, put the mug down and reach for the bear she'd left on the table.

"The last time we talked you told me to look for my compassion," he pointed out, holding the toy out to her. "I thought about what you said and you're right."

Della looked at the bear properly for the first time. It bore a tiny pink cushion with the word compassion embroidered in yellow silk.

"Do you like it?"

She nodded. "Thank you."

"I'm sorry for the way I behaved, Della. It was completely out of character for me and I guess I was in shock and—"

"It doesn't matter anymore," she said, cutting him off. She didn't want his excuses. "Isaac doesn't want to know you." Della said without apology. Isaac hadn't shown the least bit of interest in his father.

Spencer shrugged. Isaac was a grown man, he told himself, who obviously resented him for coming into his life at this late stage.

"Where's Gabbs?" he asked again.

"Out."

"I thought she'd be here, all packed up and ready to go home. I sent her a text this morning."

"No, she's not packed," Della replied, stalling.

"But she's not here?"

Spencer watched Della fidget with the toy in her hand. "Am I about to lose my temper?"

"Probably."

They used to play this game when they lived in Jamaica. They would practically confirm whatever negative emotion was going to erupt before it actually did. They'd always been able to communicate in unconventional ways.

"If you let me kiss you I promise I won't shout," Spencer floored her with that request.

"I'm not kissing you."

"Why not?"

"Because the last time you were here I was blinded by our history. We're nothing but two people who used to live next door to each other a long time ago. I don't see the need to kiss you, and I don't want you kissing me ever again."

"Can I be honest with you now that you've gotten your little speech out of the way?" he asked mockingly.

Della nodded.

"I want to be inside you right now. I want to tuck your nakedness beneath me and lose myself. I want to suckle at your breasts and touch you until you sigh my name and you make those tiny mewing noises deep in your throat. That's what I want to do to you. Right now." His voice had deepened with each word and his gaze was positively primal.

"You shouldn't talk like that," Della breathed, crossing her arms over her breasts and pressing down, trying to reduce the deep throbbing in her nipples.

Spencer simply smiled knowingly. He looked totally gorgeous in his blues jeans and white shirt. She was tempted, she really was, but their problems far outweighed half an hour of great sex. She couldn't be with a man who didn't respect her, and she certainly didn't need a sex buddy.

"Gabbriella will be here in a few minutes," she announced, desperate to switch him off. She turned her back on him and went to the kitchen to fix herself a sandwich.

\*\*\*

Gabbriella was laughing and chatting when she let herself in, but froze the moment she spied her father.

"Hi, Dad," she muttered eventually.

Spencer was looking past her, seeing his son. For a moment nobody said a word.

"Dad?" Gabbriella repeated, biting her lip.

Spencer finally looked at her, noticing the gleam of excitement in her cheeks. Her hair was pulled back in a ponytail and her face was almost make-up free. What had happened to the red lipstick and fake lashes she always wore? She was wearing a shapeless navy blue tracksuit with bright yellow trim. Isaac was wearing the same thing and a pair of sunglasses. It wasn't a sunny day.

"What's going on?" he asked them both, knowing he wasn't going to like the answer.

Isaac stepped past them and went to kiss his mother. He took a quick bite of her sandwich and headed upstairs. Della stayed in the kitchen. This was not her fight.

"I've just finished work," Gabbriella explained tentatively.

"I see."

"Isaac got me a job at his place," she rushed, as her dad did his best to digest the information. "I can only do a couple of hours for now, and I'm at the front desk. But next week I'm going to do my life-savers exam again, 'cause I didn't finish it last time down in London. And then I can move between the desk and the pool."

"I see."

Isaac bolted down the stairs and pinched the other half of his mother's sandwich before throwing a wink at his sister. He left without acknowledging his father.

"You had nothing to worry about with Isaac, Dad," Gabbriella volunteered with a smile filling the silence that was left behind her brother.

"Is that right?" Spencer said, turning to look at Della, who was doing a fine job of avoiding his gaze. "When were you going to tell me?"

"It's not my place to say," Della whispered guiltily.

"The hell it isn't!" Spencer snapped. He felt as though someone had dug a chasm in his heart with a rusty spade.

"Daddy!"

"And you," he turned on Gabbriella. "You live in London. There is nothing for you here!"

"Yes, there is. I've got my brother and I've got Della and my job and I'm—"

"You're what?"

"Nothing."

"Gabbriella?" Spencer growled.

Della quickly stepped forward and held out the little teddy bear to him. She didn't say a word.

Spencer took a deep breath and watched as his daughter moved closer to Della, twining her fingers through Della's in a symbol of solidarity that couldn't be missed. He wanted to crumble but held himself rigid. He wanted to snatch his daughter and hold her close. She was his daughter!

"Is it okay if she stays here a while?" Spencer asked past the hard lump of emotion sticking in his throat.

Della nodded.

"Thanks." With that, he turned and left.

## CHAPTER TEN

Spencer was missing. Totally off the grid. It had been two days since Della had heard from him. He had not sent any emails or used his credit cards. His mobile was off and he hadn't checked in with his office. Totally unlike Spencer. His personal assistant was frantic. Frantic enough to call Gabbriella. Frantic enough to speak to Della.

Della stared at the naked man sprawled face down on the burgundy duvet. A large gold brocade pillow covered his head and was anchored in place by two very muscular arms. Della would know Spencer's arms anywhere.

He didn't respond when she tried to wake him. He was breathing, but that was all and she sent for the hotel doctor. Spencer's skin was hot but pale and had a clammy-like sheen to it. He smelled of sickness and vulnerability and unwashed desperation. A man who had been too ill to take care of himself.

The room reeked of vomit and Della, wrinkling her nose, walked into the adjoining bathroom and found the source in the sink where she quickly turned the taps on full blast and rinsed out the curdled mess as best as she could.

She felt a heavy cloak of guilt envelop her. He shouldn't have been alone, she told herself. He could have died. A John Doe discovered weeks later in a hotel room. It was his office that raised the alarm concerning his whereabouts. That alone said a lot about his relationship with his family. It also said a lot about her.

She located his overnight bag, tipped it upside down on the carpet, and searched for something comfortable for him to wear. As tears rolled down her cheeks, she disregarded his sexy tight briefs and settled on a pair of shorts he probably used to go running in. It took her ages to get them up the dead weight of his legs, rocking his hips back and forth as she inched the loose shorts up and over his muscular thighs and taut bum. She couldn't help but notice the numerous thin white scars that criss-crossed his back and left shoulder. She'd never seen them before. What caused them? What had happened to him?

The doctor came in. He was a young, competent-looking Asian man who introduced himself as Dr. Bhandry. Together they moved Spencer to the top of the bed and made him more comfortable. Della watched anxiously as the doctor tapped this and poked that, looked down Spencer's ears and throat and listened to his chest.

Spencer's eyeballs had looked shockingly bloodshot when Dr. Bhandry lifted his eyelids. The doctor frowned as he took a penlight from his bag and moved in to look closer. Spencer mumbled something, flinched and violently knocked away the doctor's hand

Dr. Bhandry wrote some instructions for Della to follow on the hotel stationery beside the bed. He gave her his contact details and left saying something about winter flu virus and conjunctivitis.

"Spencer?" Della whispered, holding two tablets and a tall glass of water in her hand. A bellboy had brought them a white paper bag filled with antibiotic tablets, eye-drops, a small bottle of saline and a packet of cotton balls. "I need you to take these."

Spencer tried to open his eyes but the room's brightness made him flinch. Della hurriedly closed the living room door that had been letting in the harsh afternoon sunlight.

"Hold out your hands and take these," she instructed him. "The doctor said they will help with the headache."

Spencer did as he was told, and Della held the glass to his lips as he drank the water. Then, using a separate cotton ball, she carefully bathed each of his eyes with the saline solution. She gently lifted each eyelid to apply the eye-drops.

Spencer lay back with relief.

"I need to go—"

"No," he mumbled hoarsely, sliding his arm across the bed and turning his palm up to her.

She took it, curling her fingers around his and sitting down on the bed beside him.

"I'm sorry you've been alone," she whispered, fighting back tears. She'd never seen him like this.

"I need to ring Gabbs and your office. They've been worried," she told him. He gripped her fingers tighter. "I'm staying okay, but I need to make some arrangements."

With her free hand she gently stroked his cheek and smiled when he turned his face into it. "Rest now. I'm here," she said. Spencer eventually relaxed his fingers as he fell into a deep sleep. Della crept out of the room to make the calls.

***

After finishing her tasty vegetarian meal, Della took a quick shower and pulled up a chair beside Spencer's bed and propped her feet on top of the silky duvet. She was exhausted. The last few days had been marked by tending to Spencer's every need: mopping him down when his temperature crept up, holding him up when he started to vomit, and practically carrying him to the bathroom. She hadn't slept properly in days and her eyes felt dry and grainy. Making herself as comfortable as she could, she settled down to watch him sleep.

She remembered another time she had watched him sleep like this. When they were about sixteen, maybe seventeen years old, sleeping off a day of excesses. Excessive fun, sun and seafood. They'd spent the day at Alligator Pond. His brother Jeremy had had some business in the area, something about starting a safari boat tour and was looking at local attractions.

Jeremy had been in his element with the locals pathetically reverential due to his family name. He'd been flashy, loud and rude. Della had stayed close to Spencer. She'd found out too late that it was Jeremy who'd be driving down. He gave her the creeps and she wouldn't have agreed to accompany them if she had known.

It had been a nice day once Jeremy had gone. She and Spencer played Ludo with some of the fisherman who seemed relieved that Spencer was nothing like his brother. A meal of fish and lobster was prepared right there on the beach, and Della had never tasted anything so delicious in her entire life.

It was a working beach, as the fishermen caught the seafood for the whole parish, and people lined up with their brightly coloured plastic bowls to buy the catch as soon as it came in. She and Spencer had strolled hand in hand along the water's edge admiring the long bumpy shape of the Don Figueroa mountain range in the distance to which Alligator Pond got its name and not because of alligators as Della had thought. There were no alligators in Jamaica, Spencer had teased, only crocodiles.

Della remembered Spencer going for a swim in the river, but she hadn't liked the look of those ropey mangroves and dark water and she'd paddled at the waters edge, fascinated as the cold water met the warmth of the sea.

Spencer's sudden coughing made Della jump out of her thoughts. She sat up, realising he was looking at her.

"How long have you been here?" he asked hoarsely. He tried to sit up but failed.

"Two days."

He frowned. He'd lost two whole days?

"What day is it?"

"Thursday," Della told him.

Scratch that he'd practically lost a week. He felt awful, his tongue thick and furry, his head thumping as though a bunch of Irish dancers were giving a performance in his head. He attempted to swing his legs over the side of the bed.

"I'll help you up. Do you want to go to the bathroom?" Della asked.

Having to lean on Della, the effort of each step made him break into a sweat. With the door ajar, he used the toilet and looked longingly at the shower. He got up and leaned heavily against the sink, splashed cold water on his face and gargled with mouthwash. He didn't have the energy to pick up his toothbrush.

Feeling drained of all his energy, he stumbled back to the bed Della had just made up with clean sheets.

"I'll order you some soup and get you cleaned up," she said.

Della gave him a quick strip wash, and he had to think of the cold waters of the Dunns River Falls to keep himself from reacting to her touch. Now was not the time to launch his plan of seduction, he told himself tiredly. Maybe tomorrow.

*** 

Spencer was the worst kind of patient, Della decided. Why couldn't he be the 'man flu' type of guy and stay in bed? He'd spent every waking minute trying to prove he was fit and in tip-top shape. Trying to dress himself, his knees had given way and he'd ended up sprawled backwards on the bed. The look of disappointment and shock on his face was priceless, and it made Della laugh until her stomach hurt.

"Gabbriella, will stay with you tonight, I've got to go to work," she told him with nervous casualness. Over the last few days they'd talked about everything except Gabbriella and Isaac. The weekend had arrived, and Isaac had to play in the band. There was no-one to stay with Gabbriella, and Della wasn't comfortable leaving her on her own.

"I don't feel so good," Spencer coughed.

"She'll be here before I leave," Della said, ignoring him. She knew he was getting better and could manage on his own for a few hours.

"What if I fall or something?" he challenged. "She's not strong enough to help me up."

"Gabbriella is taller than me," Della pointed out. "And besides, I need to go home."

Spencer gave her a hard look. He liked having her around. Aside from feeling like death, he'd actually enjoyed these last few days. They'd talked and they'd laughed. They'd played dominoes, something he hadn't done in years. Della had even challenged him to make her a real Jamaican Ludo board. Their friendship had taken on an easy vibe, and he wasn't ready for real life to intrude. He still needed time to figure out the status of their relationship. Physically, Della was keeping her distance. Emotionally, they were re-connecting. She had loved him once. She would love him again.

"My head hurts," he said suddenly.

"Take a tablet."

"I can still hear the ringing in my ears."

Della folded her arms across her chest and looked at him with her left eyebrow raised.

"What do you want, Spencer?"

"I don't want you to go," he whispered, reaching for her hand and pulling her closer.

"We aren't friends anymore."

"Oh yeah? Then what has all this been about?" With a quick tug, he made her tumble into his lap. "You haven't left my side, and I've seen the way you've lusted after my helpless body."

Heat scorched Della's cheeks, and she dipped her head so that her hair fell forward to hide her face, but Spencer quickly pushed back the heavy curtain. Gently he cupped her face and pulled her around to face him. Their noses almost touched.

"No kissing," she objected.

He smiled a small smile. This was Della he was holding. He would never ever let her go again.

Tenderly he rubbed his nose against hers. "The definition of a kiss is something about using my lips to make a smacking sound against your skin. No smacking sound," he whispered. "No kiss."

Using his nose he nudged the side of her neck and ever so gently nipped her earlobe with his teeth. He trailed his tongue up and down the tender curve where her neck swept into her shoulder. She was wearing black leggings and a soft dress in a red and orange geometric print that came to her knees. She tilted her neck to the side, giving him better access and all the encouragement he needed. With one swift move he tipped her up, making her laugh, and repositioned her on his lap, her legs on either side of his.

He slipped his hands up her back, finding the zipper on her dress and pulling it down as far and as fast as he could. The dress sagged off one shoulder and he tugged at it, impatiently with his teeth until her breasts sprang free. She had the most beautiful breasts. Fuller than he remembered. Her nipples large, dark and inviting. He caught one in his mouth, swirling his tongue over the distended nub.

Della gripped his head and Spencer responded by bending her backwards, scooping her bottom forward so that her sex was pressed against his. She rocked into him, and with his hands steady on her hips, Spencer pushed her down hard against his throbbing erection.

Della let out that soft purring sound he loved so much and almost roughly he lifted her again, knelt on the floor with her, rolled her leggings down, nipping her inner thighs here and there as he slowly slid her knickers off along with them.

Her hands were sweeping down his shoulders to his arms and his wrists and back up again and she cried out as supporting himself on one elbow he used his other hand to dip inside her. She was swollen and ready for him.

Finding and teasing her clitoris Spencer made small, rapid circular movements with his fingers, using just the right amount of pressure to make her gasp, then down-shifting his speed making her sigh and sob with pleasure. He wanted to capture those cries but no kissing.

Spencer laughed, arching his hips away from her as she tried desperately to unbutton his jeans. He watched her closely taking her higher and higher as her hips lifted off the floor and her body began to tremble, then moving his hand he cupped her breast and fastened his mouth on the nipple sucking it deeply into his mouth. Her trembling slowed, her body relaxed and with a devilish grin he returned to her wet folds, finding the swollen nub to begin the dance again.

## CHAPTER ELEVEN

Spencer drove his titanium-coloured BMW onto the wide pebbled driveway and reversed into the space beside a navy people-carrier and turned off the engine. The female Sat Nav voice kept telling him he'd reached his destination until he eventually turned it off. This was a nice residential area, just off Mansfield road, called Mapperley Park. The trees were mature, the roads were wide and the houses had an air of timeless serenity about them. He could easily live in a neighbourhood like this.

He was early. He knew that without even looking at his watch. He had to get out of that hotel suite. Della had gone home to tend to her cat, but Spencer suspected that that was just an excuse to put some distance between them. She'd been a little quiet since Operation Non-kiss.

Gabbriella had offered to take him out to lunch, her treat, so here he was. Summoned. It was a nice day for winter. Bright, sunny and dry. Spencer got out of his car, pulled the collar of his heavy coat up to his neck and walked briskly towards the large Victorian house. The year 1886 was etched into a brick above the porch. It was a beautiful building, Spencer thought, and would have made a wonderful home. It had been converted, however, into a centre for children with learning difficulties.

Gabbriella worked here, and so did Isaac. Isaac had been keeping an eye on Gabbriella, Della had told him. Spencer wasn't too pleased with the arrangement but kept it to himself. As long as Gabbriella was happy, and he certainly couldn't refute his daughter's happiness as she was practically effervescent with it, he would keep his mouth shut.

Inside the building was airy, spacious and welcoming with sunny yellow walls and dizzying but beautiful red and yellow floor tiles that looked like original Mintons. The ceiling was high and had that old lace effect coving. Spencer was impressed. A young girl with dark hair, a narrow face and thin painted eyebrows sat behind the small front desk. He introduced himself, and she told him Gabby had just gone up the stairs to deliver a message and would return shortly.

"Is it okay if I look around?" he asked.

Sitting up, the young lady looked him up and down and pointed to a visitors' book for him to sign.

"Just don't go into any of the classrooms. The sproggs don't like to be disturbed," she said. She lacked a front-desk kind of personality, Spencer concluded.

He nodded.

"If you go up the stairs and turn left you can sit at the viewing gallery with the other parents."

"Thanks." Spencer took his time climbing the steps. He still wasn't one hundred percent well, and Dr. Bhandry had told him he'd had a rather vicious strain of flu, made worse by him being stressed and exhausted. He needed to rest. So resting he was. He was officially on holiday from the office and had begun toying with the idea of leaving altogether.

There were about eight mums, from frizzy-haired to poker straight blonde, already seated in the viewing gallery, chatting in that clicky way people do when their children have something in common. They smiled at him in welcome. Spencer sat three rows behind them, but he obviously wasn't far away enough as they turned and starting plying him with questions.

No, he didn't have a child enrolled at the centre, he answered. They looked at each other then back at him with icy suspicion. He knew what they were thinking. The days of a single man just watching children at play was over. He then found himself explaining that his daughter worked part-time at the front desk. But the interrogation—for that's exactly what it was—didn't end there. They wanted to know which girl. They all smiled and relaxed into their seats, telling him how lovely Gabbriella was. Great with the kids, they added. Spencer's heart fluttered with pride.

They quickly turned around when a series of whistles went off and a group of children ran to the centre of the gym and sat down. The children were about five or six and were each holding a bundle of brightly coloured things. When the whistle went off again, in three sharp blows, they stood up, started running around and throwing the bean bags at each other. There was more dropping than catching, but the kids were laughing and enjoying themselves.

Wearing a pair of trendy sunglasses, Isaac came into view blowing the whistle. One whistle to sit down, two whistles to stand up and three whistles to run. The kids loved it.

"Isaac is so good with my Hugo," Spencer heard one spiky blonde say, which made him lean in closer.

"Yes, Michael loves him and tries really hard to catch those bags. You know how difficult simple things like that can be for them, especially in school. At least here, they're all the same and work together," the longer-haired blonde agreed.

"Isaac's really calm and patient with the kids. I wonder if he has a girlfriend?" the frizzy blonde asked with a cheeky gleam.

"He surely makes coming here a pleasure." They all laughed but Spencer was fuming. He wanted to yell that Isaac was such a chilled out character because he was high and the sunglasses were there to mask his red, drug-induced eyes.

The class ended and Isaac, laughing and smiling with the kids, waved them off. The parents gathered their coats and left. Spencer moved closer to the large window and watched Isaac walk around with a mesh bag into which he placed the children's bean bags.

Isaac looked up and saw his dad watching him. Spencer nodded in acknowledgement and Isaac did the same.

"Hey, Dad," Gabbriella called from the doorway. "Ready?"

Spencer turned to look at his beautiful daughter. She seemed really happy here and had blossomed since she'd started the job. He turned to look at Isaac again, but he was gone.

"You feeling okay, Dad?"

"Yes. No," he amended quickly, almost forgetting his ruse to prolong the symptoms of his illness. He liked all the attention. "Just a little weak at the knees. Come on, you can buy me a juicy steak."

Gabbriella laughed. "Not on my wages, Dad," she said, threading her arm through his. "But I'll buy you a steak bake from the canteen downstairs."

\*\*\*

As promised, lunch was steak bake pies and chocolate chip muffins, eaten in the large timber-framed conservatory with a view of the back gardens. The round tables were spaced widely apart and pushed against the walls, leaving more than enough space to walk down the centre. When Spencer commented on this waste of good space, Gabbs explained that the kids found it easier to navigate the furniture this way.

Finishing the mint tea Spencer had ordered by mistake, as that could only be the reason for ordering the beverage, Gabbs took him on tour. She showed him the spacious classrooms and introduced him to every teacher and volunteer who crossed their path. She even showed him the stationery cupboard.

"You're settled, Gabbs?" he asked as they descended the stairs.

"Oh, it's great working here, Dad," she answered, looking up at him and biting her lips.

"I meant Nottingham."

"I know." Her shoulders drooped for a moment, but then she looked at him. He had to stifle a smile as he knew she was about to go into persuasion mode. "But I like it here too. It's a big enough city, tonnes of shopping and stuff, but it's small enough to not get lost in. D'you know what I mean?"

He nodded, watching the myriad of emotions crossing her expressive face.

"I love Della, Dad. She's amazing and Isaac is just letting me in. He's special."

They went past a long narrow pool that was partitioned off by a glass wall. "Because he's your brother?" he asked.

"That too. But he's talking more around me, and Della says that's a massive thing," she explained. "Isaac doesn't talk much. Della told me it will take a while for him to do that, but when you were poorly and he stayed with me, I had him laughing. And Della says that's well huge! We really connected."

Gabbs watched anxiously as Spencer made a concerted effort to fight the clenching in his stomach.

"Here we are," she breathed, referring to a secluded patio with a bunch of white plastic garden chairs. Isaac was rocking back on one, smoking a cigarette, with his feet propped up on a low wall.

"I thought we were working on that, Bro?" Gabbs said, walking up to him and holding out her hand.

Spencer watched Isaac take an extra long draw of the cigarette, tip his head back and blow out the smoke. Then, steadying the chair, he squashed the cigarette on the wall before putting the stub in his sister's waiting hand.

Isaac laughed and stood up. He lifted his arms high above his head and arched his back into a long stretch.

"You catch me, Sis."

Spencer could hear the playfulness in the boy's words. His voice was surprisingly soft. Nothing aggressive about it.

"Dad's here."

Isaac turned and the loving expression he had for his sister was instantly replaced by a blank canvas. His eyes guarded behind the blue lens of his shades.

"Hello again," Spencer said, stepping toward him and offering this hand.

"Isaac's not so big on the whole touching thing, Dad," Gabbs defended when after several seconds Isaac still hadn't moved to take his hand.

Isaac moved tentatively forward as though he was about to touch a live wire. "Is okay, Sis," he said softly. He quickly shook Spencer's hand and stepped back.

They fell silent for a moment and then an alarm sounded. Spencer searched for the source of the noise and watched as Isaac pulled his mobile phone from his pocket, looked at it and then nodded to himself.

Another alarm went off. This time from Isaac's watch. "Next class, Sis. Bye."

Spencer and Gabbs watched him go.

"He has to stick to his routine, Dad," Gabbs explained. "Or his day will get all messed up."

"How do you mean?"

"It's difficult for him." She moved to the low wall and sat on it. "Della explained it like this. Isaac always feels as though he's walking in a different direction to everybody else. So to keep in the right lane, everything is timed for him. His whole day, from wake-up to bedtime."

Spencer frowned. He watched as his son headed to his next class, bumping into a stack of floating noodles against the wall.

"Come on. My lunch time is up, too," said Gabbs, getting up. "I'll walk you out."

## CHAPTER TWELVE

Della sat on the sofa in her main living room. She was alone and Mr. Motive was on her knee. A rarity as the thought himself to dignified to do anything so feline. He'd missed her. She'd missed him too, as well as her son, her house and their routine. But what she really needed was for Spencer to go back to London and leave her alone. He was on a mission and he wasn't even trying to hide it. He wanted her in his bed, he'd told her the previous day. He wanted her in his life.

Yet he made no mention of Isaac, not once had he asked her about him of even told her his plans for Gabbriella. He obviously thought Della was supposed to slot ever so neatly into his life.

Della turned on the TV, grabbed her fleecy blanket and wrapped it over her shoulders. She wanted her old routine back. Her mobile vibrated. Della frowned as Ingrid's name flashed on the screen. She was outside, she told Della. Della didn't want to feel uncharitable, but this was the first time she'd had any peace in days and she really didn't like it when people from work came to her house. Her personal life and her work life did not overlap. Ingrid had only ever visited her once before and that was years ago.

"Sorry, Della," she said, as Della reluctantly invited her in and turned the kettle on. It was late afternoon and their rostered day off.

"What's up?" Della asked, passing Ingrid a cup of tea.

"Do you Skype?" Ingrid asked.

"Yes. Why?"

"Can I borrow it? It's just that I can't use mine at home. Bruce and the kids are there, and I need some privacy."

Della looked at Ingrid, who was just a couple of years younger than she was. Something wasn't right. Something hadn't been right for a few weeks now, and although Della had only ever met Bruce once, at last years Christmas party, she wasn't going to lie or help in Ingrid's subterfuge. They had children.

"Who're Skyping?" Della asked suspiciously. This was her house, and she didn't care if she was being nosey.

"Just a friend," Ingrid replied, staring at the cat sprawled at Della's feet.

"Male or female?"

"Female," Ingrid answered without hesitation.

"I'll get my laptop."

Della went upstairs, pulled the laptop from under her bed and took it downstairs. She'd thought about investing in one of those new tablet things but had dismissed the idea. She spent so much time on the computer at work that she found no joy with it at home. She put it on the table, opened it and turned it on.

"Here," she announced. Everything was up and running.

"Thanks, Della."

Ingrid's eyes were bright with excitement, and Della could have sworn Ingrid hadn't been wearing any lipstick when she came in.

"I'm upstairs if you need me," Della said over her shoulder as she headed for the stairs. She was going to have a shower.

It wasn't much later when she heard a knock on the front door and Ingrid talking to someone.

"Hey, Della."

Oh God it was Spencer.

Ingrid eyed Della curiously.

"We knew each other in Jamaica," Della offered. Casting a dirty look at Spencer, she excused herself to go to the kitchen. In no time, Spencer turned on the charm and had Ingrid giggling before expertly manoeuvring her out the door a few minutes later.

"That was awkward," he stated, walking towards Della with his hands in his pockets.

"You're telling me."

"You don't look too pleased."

"You blame me?" Della crossed her arms over her chest and glared at him. "Now she'll tell everyone at work that you were here."

"So?"

"So? So!" she blustered.

"It's no big deal. They were bound to find out sooner or later anyway."

"Not if I could help it, they wouldn't."

"Ashamed of me, Della?"

"Yes. Very."

The answer jolted Spencer out of his playful mood. "You're just saying that."

"I mean it. I don't want my colleagues knowing I've slept with you,"

"Oh, we've done a lot more than just sleep, Della," Spencer grinned.

"I don't want you here! I don't want you in Isaac's life!"

"You don't mean that either."

"Yes, I do!"

"I'll make you some mint tea," he soothed, trying his best to calm her down. "You're tired from looking after me all week."

"I don't want any rhatid tea!"

Spencer looked at her stunned. Della never swore, especially with a Jamaican expletive as they sounded a whole lot harsher than anywhere else in the world. "What's going on?"

Della dropped herself onto the sofa, pulled the blanket over her and buried her head in her hands. Her locks came loose and fell over her shoulders, brushing the floor.

Spencer was too scared to move and stood stiffly waiting. Eventually she looked at him. She seemed tired and upset.

"I'm sorry," he apologised before she could accuse of anything.

"No. It's not your fault. I didn't set any boundaries."

He didn't like where the conversation was heading. "I'll get you some water." He moved towards the kitchen.

"No, thank you," she stopped him. "Spencer, we really need to talk."

He turned reluctantly. She was about to break his heart again. He just knew it. "What about?"

"Gabbriella, for a start."

"What about her?"

"I love her, don't get me wrong. She's a great kid, but she can't live here indefinitely."

"Why not?"

"You live in London, for one."

"Did I ever tell you why we ended up here?"

Della shook her head.

"Gabbs was out of control. Coming home all hours, not being where she said she was going to be, lying and hanging out with the wrong crowd."

Della scoffed. "You mean being a teenager."

"No, Della. She went to private school, her classmates went on to sixth form or college. Gabbs 'forgot' to apply. Then the smoking started, and I had to lock away my drinks."

"Drinks?"

"My scotch, my brandy, my rum. Everything in my damn bar."

"Oh."

"Yes, oh. But that's not all of it. She stole a car, took it for a joyride with her friends and then crashed it!"

Della gasped in shock. "Gabbriella?"

"I drove her up here as punishment. Then you happened. We happened. And now she just wants to stay up here. She's happy, she's working and she's settled. I don't want to risk upsetting her peace, and neither do you."

"But you live in London. I work at night."

Spencer ran his hands through his hair. He was exhausted. It had been a long and emotional day.

"My house isn't very big."

He looked around. It was indeed small, but Gabbs being here gave him access to Della."I'll buy you a bigger one."

"I think we're about to have a fight, Spencer." Della stared at him.

"I don't have the energy."

He really did look a little peaky, Della noticed."For goodness sake, sit down!"

"I'm okay. No shouting. Just talk to me, Della."

"You're not buying me a house." She took a deep breath. "You've been avoiding Isaac."

Ah, so there it was at last. Nothing else really mattered. It was his non-relationship with the boy that was upsetting her.

"We're getting there," Spencer replied.

"What do you mean?"

"I spoke to him today."

"When? Where."

"I went to the centre and met them both."

Della frowned then a small smile appeared at the corner of her mouth. He'd just scored some serious points, Spencer convinced himself.

"He talked to you?"

"A bit," he said."He doesn't talk much."

"That's his dyspraxia," she explained. "Kids used to tease him in school because he would rush his words and trip all over them. He's not a confident talker."

"He and Gabbs get along well."

Della smiled again, her eyes getting all dreamy. She remembered watching how patient Gabbs was with Isaac. The girl really had a natural affinity towards people and would do well in some form of social care work.

"Gabbs caught him smoking, and she told him off."

"He was smoking?"

Uh-oh, Spencer thought. "It was his break time and he was in the patio."

"He only smokes when he's stressed out. Did he look okay? Maybe I should go up there?" Della said, looking at the clock on the wall. Rush hour would start in ten minutes.

"You're not going anywhere," said Spencer.

"Excuse me?"

"He's fine. Gabbs was planning on waiting for him, and they were going to take the bus home."

"Where's his bike?"

"He has a bike?"

"He takes it to work."

"They didn't say."

"Call Gabbs and see how they're getting home. He never leaves his bike."

"No, they're fine. He's almost twenty-one years old and perfectly able to make his way home with his sister."

"He might be twenty, but his sense of direction is worse than yours. He'll get them on the wrong bus."

Della was beginning to panic. With a dramatic sigh, Spencer took out his phone to call his daughter. Two minutes later he reported to her that Gabbs and Isaac were walking into town to have dinner and would then be walking home.

"Oh," Della responded. "When are you leaving? You're not supposed to be up and down like this. You're still recuperating."

"I'll recuperate here." With that, Spencer sat down beside her and made himself comfortable with her blanket.

## CHAPTER THIRTEEN

"I want to try and understand," Spencer said suddenly several days later. He'd just finished washing the dishes and was relaxing beside Della on the sofa.

She'd gone to work last night and was heading back out tonight. He didn't like it and was going to stop it, but in due course. One battle at a time he thought, although time was something he didn't really have.

He needed to get back to work. He needed to sort Gabbs out. He needed to connect with the boy.

"Understand what?" Della asked, yawning into the cushion she was lying on. Her eyelids felt like sandpaper against her eyeballs every time she blinked. She was fighting sleep and trying to stay awake as she had things to do like tidying Isaac's flat and sorting his things out for the week ahead.

"Isaac," Spencer replied.

Della's eyes flew open. It had been surprisingly easy for the men to avoid each other. Spencer was staying at the hotel with

Gabbriella, and Isaac would drop her off from work in the lobby.

"Understand him how?" Della asked cautiously. She wasn't in the mood to defend hers and Isaac's decision to live their life by the Livity.

"His condition."

"The dyspraxia?"

Spencer nodded as he pulled her feet from under her and began to message them with just enough pressure. Della was very ticklish.

"When was he diagnosed?"

"About five years ago."

"How?"

Della, smiling at the memory, told Spencer about that infamous trip to the supermarket, and Isaac bumping into the same man three times in the same aisle. She'd apologised profusely. Some people just thought her son was clumsy and rude.

"But he looks normal."

"That's why people find it so hard to believe he has problems," said Della. "Take him out of his comfort zone, or he gets too tired, then the testier his mood will be."

"Gabbs said you keep everything in order for him."

"I have to. He only copes when he knows what he has to do next. It hasn't been easy for him and everyday is difficult. Luckily he keeps focused and doesn't deviate from his routine at all."

"What would happen if he did?"

"His speech becomes erratic. He'll get frustrated, maybe throw a strop, and then depressed because he threw a strop."

"Does it happen very often?"

"Not so much now that he's older and we both understand his condition. He has Casey, his support worker who he sees once a month. He's got his work and he has the band."

She looked at the clock on the wall. "He'll be texting soon."

"Why? Where is he?"

"He goes cycling by the river in the early morning. Then he'll send me a text when he's home."

Spencer waited for her to invite him along, but she didn't."I'll come with you when you go," he offered.

She moved her feet. "That was nice, thank you. Where did you learn to massage?"

"My wife. She trained as a masseuse for something to do when the girls went to school."

"But I thought you met at university?"

"We did. She studied business, but all she really wanted to do was be a mum. The massage thing was to be on the side. She wanted more kids."

"She wanted more kids?"

"I was happy with three. She wanted five."

"Why five?"

"She liked large families."

"Did she come from a large family."

"Why all the questions?"

"Curious."

"She was an only child. She said her parents smothered her."

"She sounds like a nice person." Della was glad he'd found some happiness.

"She was a manipulative bitch."

Della gasped. "How do you mean?"

"I don't want to talk about it," Spencer replied, just as Della's phone beeped. "Is that him?" Spencer could see a yellow smiley face and the white gloved thumbs-up symbol on her phone.

"Yes, he's home."

"I'm coming," Spencer stated adamantly when she stood up and tied her hair back.

"Okay."

Della was pleased but hid her smile as they put on their coats and she locked the door.

"It's faster to walk," she told Spencer, as he turned towards his car.

"Walk?"

"Yes. You know that one foot in front of the other type of thing," she teased.

"It's cold."

"It's brisk and it will do you good."

"Aren't you tired?"

"This is my one bit of exercise and it's faster to cut through the alleyway than drive all the way round."

Spencer frowned down at her. Walk, but he found himself doing just that. They were silent as they made it to the top of her street, crossed the main road and meandered down narrow streets with rows of terraced houses. The alleyway she took him through was narrow, dirty and had an old sofa shoved against a rotting wooden fence.

"You walk through here by yourself?" He was not impressed.

"Spencer, I've been doing this for years. This is my neighbourhood."

"I don't like it."

"That's fine. You don't have to like it. It has nothing to do with you."

"You really believe that. Don't you, Della?" He smiled and captured her hand as he pulled her away from the broken glass she was about to step on.

"I'm not about to argue with you in the street."

"I'm not arguing, just stating a fact."

"A fact with that icy look in your eye you're trying to intimidate me with?"

"Is it working?"

She kissed her teeth. "We're here."

They'd arrived at a rectangular two-story block of flats that screamed, 'Look at me. I'm a council house building'. The brickwork was grey pebble dash and the second story had a chipped yellow metal hand rail around it. Spencer counted twelve flats.

"He's at the end," Della said as they walked through a low wrought-iron fence and along a narrow pathway.

The grounds were neatly arranged and the wheelie bins were tucked almost out of sight. The windows and doors looked like they'd recently been installed as the PVC was still an icy white.

Della knocked and let herself in.

The first thing that struck Spencer was the shadowy dimness of the room. The windows were layered in dense netting and only a determined streak of sunlight could penetrate through the heavy dark curtains that were partially drawn. The living area was open plan, with the kitchen towards the back of the room.

"I've brought Spencer with me," Della called out as she put the keys down on a side table, pulled off her coat and walked to the kitchen. "Sit down there." She pointed to a cream leather sofa and Spencer sat down and looked around.

The room was neat, tidy and minimal. He took notice of the three-seater sofa, a recliner, the table by the door and a flat screen TV squatting on a glass stand facing the sofa. Everything was pushed up against the walls, and Spencer remembered what Gabbs had said about dyspraxics needing adequate space as they weren't very good at perception. Spencer counted four clocks. Five, if you included the one on the microwave.

Della was industriously wiping down the counter in the kitchen. She looked tired, her eyes red. She'd just done a twelve-hour shift at work Spencer thought watching her now sweep the floor.

"What can I do?" Spencer offered.

"Sit down and look pretty," Della responded with a quick smile. Spencer laughed. Sometimes Della said the most unexpected things.

"Morning," Isaac said, entering the room. He was wearing grey track bottoms and a loose black t-shirt. He walked barefooted on the laminated floor and, like his mother's, his dreadlocks were tied back. They weren't as long as Della's though; they ended just below his shoulder blades and were reddish brown in colour like his sister Nicole, who he'd never met. The boy had to meet Jesse as well, Spencer knew. It was time to start getting his act together and sort out this whole mess with his children.

"Morning." Spencer stood awkwardly. Isaac went straight to his mother, gave her a kiss and picked up the mug of tea she'd just made. Then Isaac turned to him. Spencer tried to breathe through the familiar tightening in his stomach he endured whenever he was around a male Rastafarian.

"Gabbs?" Isaac asked softly.

"She's at the hotel, sleeping. We were up watching a film late last night," Spencer explained, clearing his throat. "How are you?"

Isaac stared at him over the rim of his exceptionally large mug. For a moment, Spencer thought Isaac wasn't going to answer.

"Fine."

Della listened to the exchange as she quickly prepared some cornmeal porridge and made sandwiches for Isaac to take to work. She really wanted to butt in but decided that they needed to do this on their own.

"You?" Isaac asked politely.

Della smiled proudly as she stirred the porridge. Isaac didn't do conversations, but he was at least making an effort.

"Fine, thanks." Spencer really wished Gabbs was here with her sassy gobbiness right now.

"Spencer? I'm making breakfast for Isaac, would you like something?" Della interjected.

"Coffee?"

"We don't drink coffee," Isaac said, frowning. Spencer realised this was the first time he'd seen the boy without his coloured glasses. His eyes were a light sherry brown. Spencer felt as though he was looking into his own father's eyes.

"I'll have what you have then."

Isaac continued to stare and Spencer shifted under his unnerving gaze.

"The bathroom is through there." Isaac pointed to a doorway. He hadn't said he wanted to use the bathroom, but Spencer went anyway, grateful to escape Isaac's watchfulness.

The bathroom was tiny, with dirty clothes on the floor instead of in the wicker laundry basket in the corner.

Spencer washed his hands and then did something he had never done before at another person's house. He looked in the cupboard below the sink. It had the usual things: a large tube of toothpaste, a bottle of shower gel that could be used on the body and in the hair, a clunky battery-operated shaver and an electric toothbrush. At the very back Spencer spied a can of red spray paint.

The bedroom was directly in front of the bathroom. Hearing Della and Isaac talking, Spencer tiptoed into the bedroom.

Facing the bed was a massive home-made calender that took up most of the wall. He stepped over a wet towel and walked to the calender. Each day of the week was broken down several times, from waking up to brushing his teeth to putting on his clothes to eating. Everything was timed and in detail.

Spencer looked at the bed. It wasn't made up and there was more clothes and a plate of half-eaten sandwiches on the floor. Isaac's wardrobe was a set of open shelves with the days of the week on them. Everything was in order.

"This is my room," Isaac said, coming up behind him. Spencer spun around, flushed with embarrassment that he'd been caught snooping.

"Sorry. What are these?" Spencer moved to the only window in the room to look at the trophies lined up on the windowsill.

"Trophies."

Spencer picked one up. "What for?"

"Tai Chi."

"You do Tai Chi?"

"Casey says it's to help me relax."

"Who's Casey?" Spencer asked, though Della had mentioned the name of Isaac's support worker just this morning.

"She says she's my girlfriend."

Spencer smiled, picturing a cheeky motherly type. "And is she?" he asked as he put the trophy back. There were about six of them.

"No." Isaac turned to go, but Spencer wasn't ready for him to go yet.

"I used to do Tai Chi a long time ago," he revealed. "Maybe you could take me to your class?"

Isaac frowned at him but nodded. "I have more trophies under my bed." He bent down and pulled out a large plastic box filled with trophies of various sizes.

"What do you do with this?" Spencer asked, referring to a can of neon-green spray paint.

Isaac snatched it from him and shoved the box back under the bed and walked out of the room.

"He wants me to take him to Tai Chi," Isaac said to his mother.

"That's a good idea."

"Why. He's a Chandler-Wright and they are no good."

Della closed her eyes, wishing Isaac hadn't remembered that little statement she'd uttered on a particular bad day when he was about eight years old. Isaac could remember entire conversations that took place twenty years ago, including dates and times. But ask him what he did yesterday, and he couldn't tell you without looking at his calendar.

"That's not what I actually said Isaac," Della muttered, as turned off the electric burner and spooned the porridge into a large bowl.

"You said those Chandler-Wrights treated you badly. I'm not taking anyone who treated my mother badly anywhere. Ras Simeon says I must always look after you and treat you like royalty until you find yourself a kingman."

Della cringed and avoided eye contact with Spencer. "Yes, I know that's what he said, but Spencer is your father and I said that a long time ago. Gabbriella is a Chandler-Wright and you like her, don't you?"

Isaac nodded. "She's my sister."

"He's your father."

"He didn't want us."

"That's not entirely true. He didn't know about you."

"Why not?"

Della looked at Spencer for help, but he was looking at her stonily.

"Look, why don't you eat your porridge. I'm going to whiz round with the vacuum and tidy up a bit."

"Fine," Isaac replied tightly.

Why, oh why, did he have to be in one of his moods, Della asked herself as she made up Isaac's bed, tucking the single sheet under the mattress.

It didn't take her long to tidy up the room. Isaac was a typically messy dyspraxic, and she couldn't go two days without tidying up after him. The place occasionally resembled somewhere a hurricane had passed through.

* * *

"Who's Ras Simeon?" Spencer asked casually as they walked back.

"A friend."

"What kind of friend?"

"Seriously, Spencer?"

"Seriously, Della."

"He's a family friend who looks out for Isaac."

"And you?"

"And me."

"So why haven't you mentioned him before?"

"No need." She yawned. "Are you coming in?" she asked as they reached her street.

He smiled as he took her key and opened the door for her. "No, get some sleep. I'll see you later." He cupped her cheeks tenderly with his large hands and gently brushed this thumbs along the lines of fatigue beneath her eyes.

She nodded and sleepily closed the door.

## CHAPTER FOURTEEN

"Who's Ras Simeon?" Spencer asked Gabbriella and Isaac as they sat in the little walled garden where Isaac liked to relax. It was lunch time and they had all eaten together. He'd been right, Gabbs filled those awkward silences with her constant but endearing chatter.

"Ras Simeon is my friend," Isaac answered, tipping his head back to expel the cigarette smoke. "Why?" Isaac turned to him with his dark sunglasses on and as he took another drag on his cigarette, Spencer noticed the red paint stain under the boy's index fingernail.

Della had failed to mention that Isaac liked art. It was something they could do together, Spencer thought. He used to enjoy painting and had even taken an art class once.

"You mentioned him this morning."

"You saw Isaac this morning, Dad?" asked Gabbs.

"Yes."

"Where was I?"

"Sleeping," he explained with a flicker of irritation as he wanted to get to the bottom of this other man in Della's life. "I'd taken Della breakfast."

"Nice one, Dad. You're learning."

"Thank you. Who's Ras Simeon?" Spencer asked again.

"Me and my brethren go to him to reason," said Isaac.

Spencer frowned. He knew all about these sessions. Rastafarians used reasoning sessions to justify taking drugs and discussing the perils of Babylon. Babylon being the wicked and evil West. If Spencer has his way, Isaac wouldn't be going to any more sessions.

"Mum doesn't go to those. She sees Ras Simeon on her own. He's all right."

Spencer's frown deepened. Isaac was just beginning to relax around him and he wasn't about to jeopardise their fragile relationship with an interrogation, so he kept quiet. But he was not happy. Della wouldn't be going to any more sessions either.

"What are you doing, Gabbriella?" Spencer watched perplexed as his daughter took pictures off her brother's profile.

"Every time I post a picture of Isaac on my Instagram I get another couple likes and more followers, Dad," she explained, forgetting that Spencer didn't know about her smart phone.

"And your brother doesn't mind?"

"He doesn't mind. Do you, Bro?"

Isaac grinned at his sister and Spencer saw the love flow between them. It was a love he proudly witnessed between his daughters, too.

"It helps towards her goal," Isaac explained. "She needs to reach 5000 followers for New Year's."

"To what end?" Spencer had no idea what they were talking about.

"Just because," Gabbriella shrugged. Spencer looked at Isaac to see if he would give a better explanation.

"Just because." The boy mimicked and touched his fist to his sister's.

Spencer's phone started making a strange dull beeping sound in his pocket. He fished it out and stared at it blankly.

Gabbs snatched it out of his hand and started grinning. "It's Skype calling Dad," she explained quickly as she rapidly opened the app.

Spencer didn't even know he had Skype on his phone.

"It's Jesse!" Gabbs announced.

"Hello? Jesse? Can you hear me? It's me, Gabbriella."

There was a muffled hello.

"I can't see you but I can hear you. Can you see me?" Gabbs held the phone at arm's length.

"Yes. Look at you, little sis!" Jesse said.

Gabbs laughed with tears in her eyes. "You've been gone three months already. Did you get my e-mails?"

"I was on safari so haven't been anywhere near technology. Where's Dad?"

"Here." Gabbriella pointed the phone at Spencer.

"Hi, Dad."

"Hi Sweet-pea. Where are you?"

"Kenya."

"Are you okay? Do you need any money?"

"I'm fine, Dad. How come you're all outside. I can see clouds." Gabbs turned the phone to her again.

"Guess what?" Gabbs asked animatedly, ignoring her sister's question. "Can I tell her, Dad?"

Spencer nodded.

"Jesse, we have a brother!"

"No fucking way."

"Yes fucking way!" Gabbs looked at her Dad apologetically. He gave her a stern look. "He's right here. He's called Isaac and he looks like us!"

"A brother? From where?"

"It's a long story. But I sent you an email. Actually, I sent you loads, especially when Dad was being a dad." She rolled her eyes. "D'you wanna see him? Isaac I mean. He's right here."

Gabbriella didn't wait for her sister to answer.

"Isaac, wave to Jesse. We can't see her," she explained. "But she can see us."

Isaac looked into the black square on the phone and waved self-consciously.

"How old is he?" Jesse asked.

Spencer held out his hand for his phone. He knew all too well that once the girls started talking he'd never get a chance to talk to Jesse, his middle child. He hadn't spoken to her in almost ten weeks.

"Jesse, it's Dad."

"Hi, Dad."

"We're missing you, kiddo."

"Missing you too, Dad. You look different."

"Different how?" Spencer smiled.

"Hmm, I don't know. You look a bit softer and less grouchy."

"I'm on holiday," he explained, chuckling. "Are you bored yet? Ready to come home?"

"I've just got to the Ali's, Dad," she told him. The Ali's were old friends of his who lived just outside of Nairobi. "And I've not gone to the coast yet."

"Be careful, okay? Are you still travelling with those friends you made?"

"We're meeting up again in Mombasa, and you know I'm always careful, Dad."

They were silent for a second. The last time they'd spoken they'd argued. Spencer didn't even remember what the argument was about.

"We're up in Nottingham, but I'm sure Gabbs would have told you all of that in her emails."

"We really have a brother, Dad?"

"Yes."

"How long have you known?"

"Just recently. Are you sure you're okay?"

"Yeah. I've met some lovely people," Jesse reported.

"I knew you would. I'm proud of you, kiddo, and I'm sorry."

Jesse was silent.

"Me too, Dad."

"I love you. You know that, don't you?"

"I love you, too."

"I'll put your sister back on."

"Dad?"

"Yes, Sweet-pea?"

"I do miss you."

"Rightbackatcha."

## CHAPTER FIFTEEN

The floor captain was busy talking to the tech people, the telephony people, management and whoever else commandeered the call centre when things weren't running right. They hadn't received a call in over an hour.

Ingrid was on her personal phone and was hunkered down in her chair. You could only see the top of her head. Lucia had her feet up on the desk and was finishing up her university course work. Priya was reading yesterday's paper, Jarrett was listening to music and surfing the net, and Fliss was humming to herself.

Four o'clock in the morning wasn't an easy time to be without calls. They were all struggling. They'd all be dozing off if the calls didn't start coming in soon.

"Della?" Mackenzie began, standing up and balancing his elbows on the partitions that separated his desk.

"Yes, Mac?"

"How come I can understand you like normal, and then sometimes it's like you're talking a different language?"

Fliss turned to look at her, too.

"You mean my accent?"

"Yeah. The whole mi is Jamaican, irie, no problem, ting," Mackenzie mimicked with a tinge of exaggeration.

"It comes and goes," Della explained simply. She wasn't offended.

"Didn't you leave Jamaica when you were a kid or something though?" Fliss queried, jumping onto her desk and kneeling down.

"Late teens."

"So how come your accent is so strong?" Fliss wanted to know.

"I don't really know, depends on who I'm talking to. And I'm around a lot of Jamaicans."

"My Nan is from Liverpool, and every time she goes off to see my great-aunt Sylvie I can't understand her," Lucia joined in, as she put her books away. "She sounds like a proper scouser. When I close my eyes it's like she's that girl on that stupid reality show."

They all laughed.

"I'd love to go to Jamaica to learn the lingo," Mackenzie said with a dreamy look on his face. "Hang out on the beach, drinking rum punch, and smoke ganja all day. Paradise."

"Ganja?" Lucia asked, standing up to lean on her partition. "What's ganja?"

"It's the local term for weed," Della explained. Sometimes the team could talk about the most random things.

"Ganja," Lucia uttered, mouthing the word silently a few times. She was a student of languages. "Ganja. It sounds a lot better than marijuana or cannabis"

"Yeah, marijuana sounds Spanish," said Della.

"You know the Spaniards were in the Caribbean way before the British," Lucia, who was half Spanish stated proudly. "We named everything in the Caribbean."

"I wouldn't even go there if I were you," Fliss warned. "Spanish rule and what they did to the native Taino Indians is nothing to be fucking proud of."

Everyone stared at Fliss in disbelief.

"I'd like to visit Cuba," Lucia said, breaking the awkward silence.

"Why?" Mackenzie asked with a grimace.

"All those lovely old buildings and cars. It's as though time stood still."

"It did. It was called a revolution. Castro flung out the Americans and shut the place down!" Fliss spoke so dramatically that her hoop earrings bounced against her neck.

"Oh. I forgot about that," Lucia said, pushing her long black hair behind he ears. "But I'd still like to go."

"You got family in Jamaica, Della?" Mackenzie asked, eager to take control of the conversation.

Della knew where this was heading. Mackenzie had managed to travel across America for six weeks last summer, staying with friends and friends of friends without paying a single penny for accommodation.

She thought of her house in Jamaica and the last time she had seen it. Eight large bedrooms and nine bathrooms. The sunken living room with the scattered cushions. The large pool and the pool-house that was bigger than her house here in Nottingham. It was a visitors' paradise, and Della felt a pang deep in her heart. It had been so long since she'd been home.

"No," Della said in response to Mac's question.

"Shame. I'd have loved to go play tourist up at the north coast for a bit." He put his hand on his waist and leaned to the side. "And whine mi waist like di locals." He joked, undulating his whole body suggestively.

They all laughed.

"You can't go to Jamaica, Mac," Fliss scoffed a moment later.

"Why not?"

"You're too gay."

"What!"

"Anyone can look at you and tell."

Mackenzie puffed out his chest.

"I'm not gay!" he defended. "I just have too much X chromosomes."

Fliss laughed.

"It's true! My mother was under a lot of stress when she was preggers with me."

"And that makes you gay?"

"I like women," Mac replied tightly through his teeth.

"And men," Fliss added.

"Felicity, leave the man alone. He is what he is," Della interrupted before they really started to argue. Fliss could reduce a man to tears with her mouth alone. And Della was too tired to play referee tonight and shifted lower in her chair.

"I don't like Jamaica," Lucia admitted, jolting Della out of her pensive mood.

"Why not? Everyone likes Jamaica. It's the most popular country in the Caribbean, if not the world," noted Mackenzie, obviously scandalised. "It gave us reggae."

"So? It's too violent."

"That's just the media," Della replied.

"Sorry, Della, but you haven't been there in years," Lucia said. "I saw this documentary the other day, and it said Jamaica had one of the highest murder rates in the world."

"And I saw that same documentary, and it explained it was something to do with the square foot ratio between two neighbouring gangs. That's why it's so high," Fliss interjected.

"Doesn't matter. It's still high."

"Lucia, you can be such a frigging prima donna sometimes," Fliss jeered as she jumped off the desk and walked around. She forgot to remove her headset, and it was yanked off her head and went flying back to her desk with a clatter. "The Western media wants you to believe you'll get shot as soon as you leave your hotel," she continued, unfazed, scooping up the headset.

"And I won't?"

"Course you won't," she said, putting her headset back on. "This government doesn't want us to spend our money outside the Union. That's why they're putting that luxury tax thingy on all long-distance travel."

"How the hell do you know all this stuff, Fliss?" Mackenzie asked, voicing what everyone else was thinking. "I'd still go, grow my dreads and just chillax with the Rastas."

"You think having dreads makes you a Rasta, Mac?" Della asked softly.

"Yeah," he smirked. "And the weed."

"I've been a Rastafarian for many years, and I don't smoke weed. Never have."

"I smoke weed all the time."

"Why?"

He shrugged. "It takes me to another place. I can almost turn myself inside out and have a conversation with my soul."

"And you need to smoke to do that?"

"It's either that or get drunk, Della. Which would you choose?" He flashed his blue eyes angrily.

"I'm not judging you, Mac. It's just that most people don't understand what being a Rasta is all about." She thought of Spencer and his attitude towards the movement. "It's almost spiritual, a way of life in which you learn to love all things equally. There is a peacefulness inside me that I never had until I became a Rasta."

"When did you become one, Della?" Lucia asked curiously.

"About twelve or so years ago."

"But how do you become one? I mean I was baptised Catholic because that's what my family is. How and why did you become one?"

Della smiled and stood up so she could see them all properly. She moved the voice tube away from her mouth and turned it so that it was near her ear and out of her way. "It took years of staying focused and meditating to get rid of everyday negative noise. Rastafari was in my heart anyway. There aren't any rules or rituals we have to adhere to. Our ultimate goal is for peace, love and unity in this world."

"And that's it?" Mackenzie looked disappointed.

"People are attracted to it because it's simple."

"So why the association with ganja?" Lucia asked.

"Some Rastas use it to clear their head and to take them to a higher place. As I said, not all Rastas smoke it. Not all Rastas are strict vegetarians, and you don't have to have dreadlocks to be a

Rastafarian either."

Mackenzie looked crushed.

"Anyway, Mac. It would take you years to grow dreads," Della teased, wanting to lighten the mood.

Mackenzie looked at her and seized the opening she had given him. He laughed heartily, reminding them of his lovable side.

"I'd do it just to piss my parents off," he said, thumping his muscular chest. "A blonde dreadlocked eco-warrior driving up and down the A52 looking for road kill."

"Eww!" Lucia said.

"Disgusting!" Fliss joined.

"Pheasant, anyone?" Mackenzie teased.

## CHAPTER SIXTEEN

The last time Della had seen Spencer this excited was the day of his eighteenth birthday party and she knew just how well that turned out she remembered sardonically.

Spencer was making them laugh with stories of their childhood, wildly exaggerating most of them but Gabbs and Isaac didn't know that.

"Right," Spencer started as soon as Isaac swallowed his last bit of creamy sweet potato mash. "Let's go." He threw down his napkin and stood up eagerly.

"Dad, seriously?" Gabbriella looked at him, confused. "You're beginning to creep me out."

Spencer laughed and put his arm over his daughter's narrow shoulders, pulling her close as he led them out of the hotel's restaurant.

"Upstairs. All of you," he ordered, releasing Gabbriella to shepherd them towards the bank of lifts. They waited for Isaac, who was lagging behind and looking at the front entrance as though wanting to make a run for it. Spencer walked back to him. The two men stood looking at each other. Isaac was wearing green-tinted glasses.

"I've got a surprise for your mother," Spencer said, "and I'd like you to be there with us. As a family."

Spencer was well aware that if it wasn't for Gabbriella, Isaac probably wouldn't have joined them at dinner. But he knew he wouldn't refuse this final request.

Isaac nodded and together they silently walked to the lift Della was holding open for them.

Spencer opened the door to his suite with a flourish. He'd rearranged the furniture so that four waist-high black speaker boxes and a high table with two turntables dominated the room. The room was completely different from the last time Della had seen it. He'd even got a mini disco ball rolling around madly on a small stand, throwing red and green lights onto the walls and ceiling.

"Dad, are you going through some mid-life crisis or something, cause this is freaking me out big time," Gabbriella said as she walked to the table, pulled out her phone and started taking pictures.

"D'you like it?" Spencer asked Della, ignoring his daughter who was putting on his new headphones and fiddling with the mixer between the turntables. The living room was now a DJ's paradise.

"You'd always wanted your own sound system," Della said softly, remembering all the plans he'd had of making money by playing at parties and school fêtes around Kingston.

"I went for a walk this morning and found myself on that road just up there, with the brilliant graffiti on the lamp-posts," he said, gesturing in the general direction. "Alfaton Road?"

He'd had the best day, walking up Maid Marian Way, past the Gala Casino and St. Barnabas Cathedral. Every now and then he came across a lamp-post painted with graffiti. The detail was incredible. He walked past Kemet FM, the local radio station he'd taken to listening to whilst in Nottingham. The area showed off its cultural diversity like a banner for the United Nations.

It wasn't until he'd crossed the street that he saw it. There it was, squashed between a halal butcher shop and a Polish convenience store: a record shop full of reggae, calypso and dancehall music. Heaven on Earth.

Unable to make up his mind, he offered the owner an eye-watering amount of money and bought 16 crates of original vinyls, which dated from 1970 to 1990.

"Alfreton Road," Della corrected, snapping Spencer out of his flashback. She usually shopped in that area once a month, getting her yams, dasheens and plantains.

Spencer walked to one of the crates by the wall and pulled out two records sporting white sleeves. "Do you know how long it's been since I've been in a record shop?" he asked excitedly. "Sit down there." He pointed to the sofa, walked to the turntables and shooed Gabbriella away with a flick of his wrists. "Listen to this, Della."

He threw a grin at his daughter, who was looking at him as though he'd morphed into another person right before her eyes.

"Watch your dad mix, Gabbs," Spencer teased.

Spencer shook out his shoulders and moved his neck from side to side and ear to shoulder a few times. Then, wriggling his fingers, he put a record on each turntable, wedged one headphone between his ear and shoulder and began to play.

He was amazing to watch, very much at home behind the turntables, Della thought, as Spencer effortlessly flowed from Junior Reid's *One Blood* to Tenor Saw's *Ring the Alarm*.

Back in Jamaica, they had spent quite a few Saturday mornings buying records at Derrick Harriott's shop in Half-Way-Tree. Music had always provided a soundtrack to their lives. But one day the music suddenly stopped.

"Do you remember this, Della?" Spencer asked, putting on an extended version of *Surround Me with Love*. He dashed around the table to pull her to her feet.

"Hmm hmm. Cynthia Schloss, I think?" Della replied as he pulled her close. "You know Gabbs thinks you've gone crazy, don't you?" Della whispered in Spencer's ear.

Gabbriella and Isaac looked at each other and smiled, watching their parents hold each other close and swaying to the lover's rock groove that was playing.

"She thinks I was born a man and never had a childhood."

Della giggled and looked up at him, seeing him as a seventeen-year-old. "This is nice."

"Hmm hmm," he echoed. "Holding you again is nice." Spencer buried his face into the side of her neck and breathed in the scent of her. He'd missed her so much when she'd left him.

"Remember I went to your school fête and we danced this in the hall?" he asked.

"We had some fun times back then, didn't we?" said Della. She'd been so happy when he'd turned up at her school, even though his snobby friends had been horrified, but Spencer didn't care. He never cared what people thought and never judged anyone for being who they were. He treated everyone as his equal. What or who had changed him so much?

"We can have it again," he whispered, cupping her face in his large hands and brushing her soft lips with his thumb.

Della smiled sadly, shook her head and stepped away from him.

Spencer let her go and watched as she walked over to one of the crates, sat on the floor and began to sift through it.

"Do you want to try, Isaac?" Spencer asked the boy and held out the headphones.

\*\*\*

"Can you drive, Isaac?" Gabbriella turned to look at her brother who was rocking back on the plastic garden chair and smoking a cigarette. It was cold and she had on several layers, as well as a very furry hat with flaps to cover her ears. Isaac was just in his tracksuit.

"I did go for my test a few times, but never get through."

Gabbriella grinned. "How many times?"

"Twenty-three times."

"Twenty-three times!"

Isaac didn't look the least bit embarrassed as he took another draw on his cigarette.

"What'd you fail on?"

"Turning left when them say right mostly."

"That's it?"

"I get mixed up with my right and left."

"What hand do you write with?"

"This," he replied, putting up his right hand, the cigarette between his fingers. "And this." He showed his left.

"You're ambidextrous?"

"If you mean I can draw with both my hands, then yes."

"Coolios." She smiled at him. "Don't tell, Dad, but I can drive," she revealed, "but I don't have a license."

"How did you learn?"

"Me and my friend Malina used to borrow her mother's car at night."

"Steal it you mean?"

"No, borrow."

Isaac frowned. "With permission?"

"She was sleeping and wouldn't have minded anyways."

"So you took it?"

"Listen," Gabbs said, getting annoyed. "We borrowed it, drove around with our friends for a bit then parked it exactly as she'd left it. She never knew."

"I don't like them kind of things, Sister."

"It's not for you to like though, is it?"

"So why you just don't get your license?" Isaac asked.

"Don't know." Gabbriella shrugged, looked at the phone in her hand and started to scroll through it before looking up quickly. "You won't tell Dad?"

Isaac tipped his head back to blow out the cigarette smoke. He rubbed the cigarette butt against the sole of his trainers to put it out before answering. "No," he said eventually. "It's not like me and him are friends."

"Thanks."

"But don't do it again," Isaac warned. "You could hurt yourself or somebody."

"Yes, sir!"

## CHAPTER SEVENTEEN

"What have you done?"

Della approached Spencer as he got out of a white panel van, with the name of his hotel splashed in gold lettering on the side, and slammed the door.

"They kicked me out," he admitted reluctantly.

"Sorry?"

"You heard me," he growled, looking everywhere but at her. "They kicked me out of the hotel!"

Della frowned as she opened her front door.

"Where have you been?" Spencer asked tightly as he tracked her to the kitchen slinging his suit bag onto the sofa along the way. He'd been waiting for over an hour for her. She should have been at home.

"Sorting Isaac's flat," Della answered.

"Why?"

"It's what I do," she replied, matching his tone. "What did you do?"

"Apparently," he seethed, crossing his arms over his chest. "There were complaints about my noise."

Della looked at him and blinked twice, thinking she'd heard

wrong. The expression on his face was priceless and she couldn't stop the laughter from bubbling up her throat. Tears filled her eyes and spilled onto her cheeks as she doubled over with laughter but stopped with a hiccup when he spun on his heel, went to the van, dragged out a large box and dropped it with a thud of permanence on her white carpet.

"And where do you think you're going with that?" Della asked, stunned, as he reached inside the van again and dragged out a leather rucksack.

"I'm stopping with you."

"I don't think so," Della said to his back, but he was already back at the vehicle and emptying it of his luggage and boxes. He piled everything inside the room. "You can't stay here!"

"I'll have to until I sort something out."

"You've got a lot of sorting out to do, Spencer Chandler-Wright. But you'll have to do it some place else. I haven't got room for you."

Spencer nudged the front door shut with his foot and stepped around a crate of records.

"Are we about to have a fight?" he asked, placing his hands on his denim-clad hips.

She looked beautiful, standing there, even though her eyes were spitting rockets at him as she tried to look stern. Spencer knew he could simply pick her up and tip her over to make her laugh. She used to love the way he would carry her over his shoulder and off to bed.

"Don't you dare," she warned, putting her arms out in front of her. Spencer quickly trapped her between a large black speaker and Gabbriella's bags.

"Don't worry. I'm not going to kiss you," he whispered. "No kissing, remember?" He ran his tongue down the length of her neck just behind her ear.

A zingy sensation coursed through Della all the way to her nipples. She felt them swell uncomfortably against her bra.

Spencer leaned his body into hers and cupped her face. She looked at him, her mouth slightly open, her eyes slightly closed and her breathing light.

"You can kiss me," Spencer whispered just a breath away from her lips.

"No."

"You can." He brushed his lips ever so gently against hers. "I won't tell anyone."

She giggled, forgetting she was supposed to be mad at him.

Spencer shifted so that he could reach her long hair. He wrapped some of the heavy strands around his fist, pulling gently until her neck was open and vulnerable to his mouth. Using his teeth, he gently nipped his way down to her collarbone, skimming the tip of his tongue along the gentle ridge until he reached the shallow vee at her throat. Della whimpered and raised her chest invitingly up to him. He growled deep in his throat.

Della was wearing her uniform of boots and black leggings, with a skinny black jumper under a colourful dress. Releasing her hair, Spencer urgently pushed her dress and jumper up her body, bundling them under her chin and sighing as his hand finally found the smooth warm skin of her stomach. But it wasn't enough.

"Kiss me," he ordered roughly. As he spun her around, whipped the dress over her head and sat her on the speaker.

"No."

"So stubborn."

Spencer caught the hem of her jumper and quickly lifted it over her head. It got stuck in her hair so he left it there, turban style, and pulled her to the edge of the black speaker box. Supporting her back with one of his muscular arms, he scooped her breasts out of their cups to suck first one nipple and then the other deep into his mouth.

Spencer with a glint in his eye watched her as he skimmed his hand down her stomach to dip into the waistband of her leggings where he cupped her sex, pressing upwards as she pressed down onto his hand.

"Kiss me."

"No," she panted.

Spencer smiled as he watched her close her eyes. The trembling in her body was about to begin. But with a smile of her own Della closed her legs and sat up to grab the waistband of his jeans, jerking him closer to undo the button. She pulled down the zipper ever so gently and rolled his jeans and briefs down until they reached his thighs.

His penis was hard and inviting and tantalisingly close to her mouth. Della looked up at him, a small smile playing at the corner of her mouth. She wrapped her hand around him, breathing in the deep musky scent. She leaned in closer, ready to take him, but he shifted away and shook his head.

"I can't wait." Spencer swiftly pulled down her leggings and knickers as far as they could go, ignoring her boots. Stepping into the circle her legs made, he pulled her to the very edge of the box. Her legs were wrapped tightly around his waist, as he pushed into her with one smooth and blissful move.

Inside her felt like heaven, small, wet and tight. Her muscles grabbed and released him, picking up his rhythm as he moved rapidly inside her.

As Della tried her best to hold back and control her breathing, Spencer did what he'd thought of doing earlier. He hoisted her up so high that her hips were off the speaker box, her legs still firmly entwined around his waist.

He moved as deeply as he could and watched with carnal satisfaction as she let out a primal scream. Her body continued to tremble as he climaxed and his essence joined hers.

* * *

"Did I hurt you?" Spencer whispered, as he slipped out of her and bent to pull up his boxers and trousers in one smooth movement.

"No." Della jumped off the box and adjusted her clothes. She'd never felt so embarrassed in her life. This was not supposed to happen again.

"You kissed me," she stated flatly.

"I did."

Della looked past him, seeing all the crates that were now occupying her lovely white room. One of Spencer's boxes was leaning against her white silk-and-lace curtains, stretching the delicate fabric from the pole. She'd saved so hard for those curtains. This room was her one and only place of peace and tranquillity and its present state moved her to tears.

"Hey," Spencer said gently. "What's the matter?"

She flicked a tear away. "This shouldn't have happened, Spencer," she said. "And I'm not feeling too good about myself right now." She tried to move past him but he caught her hand.

"Talk to me, Della," Spencer urged softly.

She shook her head and pulled away from him, moving towards the stairs. She stopped suddenly and turned back to him.

"I didn't want this." She waved her arm around the room, indicating all the bags, crates of records and boxes of sound equipment. Then she raised her small chin and looked him directly in the eye. "I didn't want to sleep with you again. It doesn't feel right to me. It goes against my values, and I don't really want you."

"You don't mean that."

"Yes, Spencer, I do," she whispered. "You come along and take over. I said Gabbriella couldn't stay here. And as much as I love her, I value my own space. I've spent the last twenty-one years being a single parent to a boy who was difficult, violent and compulsive. And me having to deal with the police on my doorstep more than once."

"Violent?" Spencer said, sounding surprised. "Police?"

"Before he was diagnosed. It was hard," she told him, remembering the fights and the bad company Isaac used to keep. "It was a living hell."

"Violent towards you?"

"No!" Della exclaimed, turning around to face him. "Isaac isn't like that anymore. But you don't get it. You don't understand."

"Then help me to understand," Spencer pleaded.

Della took a deep breath, as if she were a diver about to leap into the unknown.

"I don't want a relationship," she said. "I don't want to share my house. I want to come home from work and fall asleep on the sofa if I want to. I'm just getting back to me after all these years, learning who I am and I'm enjoying the silence."

"But I'm not taking that away from you."

"Yes, you are! You're here asking me where I've been, as though I'm accountable to you!"

"And that's unreasonable? To care about you're well-being?"

"It's not just that!"

"Then what?"

"You're trying to take over."

Spencer ran a hand through his hair as he tried to understand.

"Della, you and I go way back. You play the starring role in my happiest memories. I want to take care of you. I want to take some of the burden from you."

"But I never asked you to."

"Damn it woman! I only want to make life easier for you."

"Why, Spencer?"

"What the hell do you mean why?"

"Why, when your own family life is such a mess?"

Spencer pulled himself up to his full height.

"Isaac and I are doing just fine," Della said passionately. "But Gabbriella practically ran away from you. And you've not spoken about or spoken to your daughters since you've been up here." She paused. "You should be at work. You have responsibilities, yet you spend your days playing music, bothering me and getting kicked out of hotels! What's that about?"

"Enjoyment?" Spencer smothered the smile that was threatening to appear. "And it was only one hotel," he added sheepishly.

"You've been trying to recapture that time when we were young and carefree. It's almost as though you've reverted to life as a teenager again."

"So? You were supposed to spend the rest of your life with me. You promised. I've found you. We're back together and we have a son."

Della gasped. He just didn't get it.

"Spencer, we aren't together," she told him.

Spencer literally rocked back on his heels. It was the first time Della had seen him do it.

"So what has the last few weeks been to you?"

Della couldn't look at him. She didn't have an answer. But their affair wasn't sitting well with her morals.

"This is me, Della," Spencer pleaded. "You used to know me better than I know myself."

"But not anymore."

"Nothing has changed."

"Yes, it has. The Spencer I knew wouldn't ignore those closest to him. You've been hiding up here when you have to sort out your life. Gabbriella needs stability. Your other daughters don't even know about Isaac yet."

"I spoke to Jesse the other day," Spencer pointed out. "She met him over a video call."

"And that's supposed to make me feel better? What about your life in London? Where does Isaac fit?"

"I'm figuring it out, Della!"

"But why aren't you trying to get to know him better?" Della pushed.

"It's not like I've not been trying." Spencer tried to hold onto his temper. "But how the boy gets anything done when he's always high is beyond me!"

Della gasped.

"He's not always high! How dare you!"

"Every day he has to hide behind his fancy glasses to hide his red eyes. I've seen them!"

"Get out!" Della balled her hands into tight fists to keep from slugging him.

"Don't be stupid."

"Don't you call me stupid." She began to shake.

"I'm calling the situation stupid, not you!"

"I want you to leave."

"And go where exactly?"

"I don't care."

"What about my stuff?"

"Spencer, please," she sighed, shaking her head. "Go back to London."

Spencer refused to believe his ears after everything that had happened between them over the past few weeks. It had been beautiful. He'd never been happier, and she was happy too.

"And Gabbriella?" he asked tightly. "You want me to just pluck her from her job and expose her to the same negative environment that kept getting her into trouble?"

"She's your daughter." Della hated herself for saying it.

"But she's formed an attachment to you," Spencer announced. "An attachment you've been encouraging!"

Della shook her head. Spencer wasn't getting it.

"You have until the weekend. Then I want all of this gone," she said.

"Not happening," he answered stubbornly, folding his arms across his chest. "What's the point in going back to London when it's going to be Christmas in a few weeks? I'm not moving her before I have to!"

"You see, you haven't even asked me my plans. You just assume me and Isaac will fall in with yours."

Spencer took a deep breath and tried to calm down.

"Okay. What are you doing for Christmas?" He posed the question in what he hoped was a decent voice, though he really wanted to shout. Did Rastas even celebrate Christmas?

"It's none of—"

Spencer cut her off with his mouth. To hell with her no kissing foolishness. He had to stop her from saying something he knew she'd regret. His lips moved over hers savagely as he picked her up and braced her against the wall. He swirled his tongue inside her mouth until he felt her resistance melting.

What's happening to me? Della asked herself. She was not like this. She was a calm woman, an earthy woman. She didn't do passion. She didn't do casual sex. She took comfort in her routine and in looking after her son.

"No!" She pressed her hands against his chest and pushed him away. "No more."

There was a knock at the door.

Della looked at her watch. Neither Isaac nor Gabbriella were expected home yet, and she wasn't expecting anyone else.

Straightening her clothes, she moved towards the door, but Spencer beat her to it.

"It's for you," he announced over his shoulder. She flashed him a look that said, who else?

Della didn't expect to see Ras Simeon, but there he was.

"Good morning, Ras Simeon."

"Blessed morning, Empress."

\*\*\*

Ras Simeon was dressed in a long brown tunic trimmed with red, green and gold bands at the cuffs. His dreadlocks were bundled up in a black woolly tam with red, green and gold streaks. She'd never seen him dressed like this before. What was going on, she thought. She opened the door wider and invited him in with a puzzled look.

"Ras Simeon, this is Spencer, Isaac's father," Della said reluctantly, before speeding off to make some tea. The two men shook hands.

This was not how Spencer expected Ras Simeon to look. The man was tall, with a long and narrow face. His beard was neatly trimmed and his skin dark and smooth. Unfortunately for Spencer, he wasn't ugly.

Did Della find this man attractive? Spencer pondered the question for a minute, then quickly dismissed it. She didn't. She may go to Ras Simeon for emotional and spiritual support, but he had been her one and only lover. And from now on, he'd also be the only man she'd be going to for emotional support. He watched as she walked back into the room, doing a fine job of avoiding eye contact with him.

"I'll be back for these later," Spencer said, stacking several crates together. He turned to shake Ras Simeon's hand and then planted a kiss full on Della's already swollen lips. He then let himself out with a satisfied smile. Della couldn't be more his, he convinced himself, and now Ras Simeon knew it too.

## CHAPTER EIGHTEEN

Della hated that it got dark so early she thought as she searched for her coat. Four-thirty five and all the street lights were on trying to push the blackness away with spots of amber on the pavement. Her days seemed extra long this time of year, too. By the time she slept and woke up, it was already dark. It was depressing.

She also saw less of Isaac, but she was glad he and Spencer were spending a lot of time together. Spencer had rented a house in Mapperley Park, which was near enough for Isaac and Gabbriella to walk to and from work. Isaac had even stayed overnight a few times.

Whatever Spencer was doing it was working. Both Gabbriella and Isaac were bonding with their dad, and Della was pleased.

Christmas was two weeks away, and they hadn't made any plans. Gabbriella had yet to speak to her dad about her future and Della was reluctant to speak on her behalf. Spencer wasn't going to be pleased. Then again, who knew? The Spencer who was hanging around these days was a lot more likeable than the controlling bully from weeks back.

He must have really thought about their relationship and was respecting the space she needed, Della concluded. She was grateful, but now that he wasn't pursuing her as ardently as she would have liked, things felt a bit strange.

Della picked up the two bags of groceries she'd left in the living room. An orange fell to the floor and rolled away. She scooped it up and shoved it back into the woven Bag for Life she used. She let herself out, locked the door and headed up the street. She had to work tonight, but had stopped at the mini supermarket before going home, knowing Isaac would be running low on food.

He hadn't text-messaged her as he usually did, and Della was trying not to worry. She knew he was leading his own life and this new independence was great, but no matter what, he was supposed to text his thumbs up symbol. That's all she asked, and she'd told him time and time again to just do that one little thing so she'd know he was coping and was okay. She'd definitely be telling him off when she saw him.

Patches of black ice were everywhere and the fog was getting thicker. Their closeness to the river made the neighbourhood more prone to fog than most parts of the city. Although it was early, nobody was about and Della could hear her own footsteps as she walked towards Isaac's flat. She decided that she'd make some soup for him to take to work later in the week. She didn't allow Isaac to cook for himself, as he was too forgetful. So she either made his meals or he'd buy something.

 Della was so busy musing she didn't realise she'd reached the shadowy bit in the alley until she felt the presence of someone behind her and turned around.

All she could make out was the triangular point of a hood and dark clothing. It was a slim individual. It could have been a girl, as they were getting as bad as the boys these days.

"Gimmi your bag right," the person demanded in a deep Nottinghamshire accent. It was a young lad, Della realised.

"I don't have one," Della replied bravely.

This was her neighbourhood and everyone knew her. They also knew not to mess with her. What was wrong with this kid?

"Gimmi that then, right." Hoodie Boy flashed his hand around and

Della saw the glint of a small serrated kitchen knife. The kid meant business.

"Here." She wasn't going to risk her life over twenty pounds worth of supermarket food.

She swiftly set down the bags on the ground.

"You got a purse or watch or summut?"

"No."

"Fucksakes," Hoodie Boy breathed. "Empty your pockets."

The kid was getting antsy. He must be on drugs or was drunk, Della thought. His movements were jerky and his speech slurred.

She did as he asked but obviously not fast enough, as he grabbed her and roughly pushed his hands into one of her coat pockets and then the other. He wasn't much taller than she was, and he smelled of wine, cigarettes and mushy peas.

"Open your coat then, innit," Hoodie Boy ordered, looking up and down the alley.

She did as he commanded. She didn't have any money with her and told him so.

"Right then. Walk that way and don't you look back, right," he ordered. Feeling relieved, Della turned in the direction of Isaac's flat but then appearing out of nowhere, a group of noisy girls entered the alley from behind them and Hoodie Boy jumped nervously, shouted at them to fuck the hell off and shoved Della to the ground at the same time. The girls screamed and ran off. Della could hear the tat, tat, tat of spindly high heels running away.

She hit the dirty ground hard, banging her head on the concrete. An orange had escaped from the bag and she watched as it rolled away slowly and bump gently against the fence. Hoodie Boy started to laugh. It was a strange sound that reminded Della of a wailing alley cat about to fight.

Hoodie Boy bent towards her. She didn't know what he was doing, but she could feel the warmth of his stale breath on her cheek. He was there forever it seemed, and she closed her eyes as she didn't want his face to be the last one that she saw.

He laughed again and gave her a vicious kick in her stomach

before running off.

\*\*\*

The paramedics were being so gentle, Della thought, looking up into the eyes of a blue-eyed blonde man with red facial hair. He had kind eyes. A dark-haired woman was standing beside him, and together they opened her coat, saying something about two stab wounds to the abdomen.

Della couldn't remember getting stabbed. She didn't feel any pain and just wanted them to fix whatever they needed to fix so she could go and make the soup for Isaac.

"Stay with us," Mr. Kind Eyes said.

She smiled.

"That's my girl. We're off to Queens Med now, sweetheart. You just hold on."

Yes, she was going to hold on to that lovely cloud that was hovering just above her head. She reached out to touch it.

\*\*\*

"Everyone on meeting please." Surprised at the order, the whole team turned to look at their floor captain. They were just about to start their shift.

Monica-Louise stood closest to Jarrett, her hand on his shoulder, and everyone could see the distress in her eyes.

"Della was stabbed today," she whispered, through the emotion that was sticking in her throat.

There was a general gasp from everyone.

"How? Where? What happened?" Fliss stood up and looked around.

"Going to her son's house. It happened this evening. Mr. Chandler-Wright rang me at home." For once her voice wasn't dripping with self importance.

Everyone loved Della.

"She was stabbed twice and bled out for a bit." Tears welled up in

Monica-Louise's eyes and ran down her cheeks. "It was a mugging gone wrong."

"How is she?" Lucia asked softly, turning in her chair to cling to Ingrid.

"She was found pretty quickly and no major organs were compromised. She's expected to make a full recovery."

"Which hospital is she in?" Mackenzie asked.

"Queen's, but Mr. Chandler-Wright said no visitors please."

"That's bullshit! Of course we're going to visit!" Fliss exclaimed, saying what they all were thinking. "Who is he to tell us not to visit? She's our mother!"

"He's her partner," Ingrid said through tears while gently stroking Lucia's hair.

"What?" Mackenzie said. His face was red and he was holding himself rigid, trying to keep his emotions out of sight. He'd never looked so manly.

"They knew each other in Jamaica. I was at her house one day and he came round."

Everyone fell silent as they digested this last bit of news. They felt betrayed but tried not to dwell on it, knowing Della was lying in a hospital bed suffering from stab wounds. Della had always been private, but it still felt like a betrayal.

"He can't tell me what I can and can't do!" Fliss said defiantly. Fliss loved Della, who was like the mother she'd always wanted, caring and non-judgemental. "I'm sorry," she continued, turning to Monica-Louise. "I can't stay tonight."

The floor captain could see that she was genuinely upset. She knew Fliss and Della had a special relationship. Della had pleaded with Monica-Louise more than once to give the young girl another chance.

"Now everyone," Monica-Louise began. "I know this is a shock, but we've got work to do. I think Della would really appreciate some flowers, so I'll do a whip round later."

They all nodded in agreement.

"Now let's get selling. Our Della could really do with that exotic prized holiday to recuperate, even if it is Benidorm!" she joked before turning to Fliss. "Come with me."

Fliss took off her headset warily and followed the floor captain to her station in the middle of the floor.

"I know how important Della is to you," Monica-Louise said gently. "You can go. I'll put you down on compassionate leave so you'll still get your commission."

Fliss floundered for a moment. This act of kindness was totally unexpected, and her eyes filled with tears again.

"Thank you."

"Give Della our love from us all."

Fliss smiled, got her things and walked out.

## CHAPTER NINETEEN

"Where's your brother?" Spencer walked into the living room and dropped himself into the recliner, balancing his beer on his knee.

Gabbriella was sprawled backwards on the long sofa with both legs propped up on the back and her head over the edge. Her curly hair was loose and brushing the carpet. Spencer shook his head. She didn't look comfortable.

"He went out," she said, fiddling with her earphones.

"Didn't I say to watch him?"

Gabbriella took out one earplug and sighed. Spencer could still hear the din of her music. "He said something about going to see Ras Simon, or some name sounding like that."

"Turn that damn thing down before you go deaf! Ras Simeon?"

Spencer watched as his daughter did some sort of gymnastic manoeuvre before sitting upright again in seconds. Her face was flushed red and her hair was sticking out in all directions. Spencer tried not to smile.

"That's it. Simeon."

"And you just let him go?"

Gabbriella shrugged. "You weren't here and he said he'll be back soon. He goes once a month."

This was precisely what Spencer didn't want. The boy was hanging about in a room filled with weed smoking elders, talking about the perils of Babylon and repatriation to the Motherland.

"Do you know where he goes?"

"'Course. I've been with him."

"Excuse me?"

"Chillax, Dad. We went after work one day 'cause Isaac needed to pick up something."

"What?"

"Huh?"

"What did he need to pick up?" Spencer could feel the tension in his shoulders mounting.

Gabbriella shrugged and with a loud tut slid her finger across the screen of her device to wind her earplugs around it with a show of reluctance. "Something in a plastic bag, Dad. I don't know what."

"Get your coat."

"Why?"

"We're going to get him."

"Coolios." Gabbriella got up and stretched her arms high over her head. "Can we get some dinner 'cause I'm starving. There's nothing here to eat."

"I left you some money."

"I spent it."

"Gabbriella," Spencer sighed as he walked out to the hallway and put on his coat before grabbing his keys from the table.

"It's walking distance, Dad," Gabbs told him as they walked past the car.

They headed down the long driveway, and Gabbriella tucked her arm around his and snuggled in close.

"How's Della doing?"

"Better. She'll probably be coming home tomorrow or the day after."

"Coolios." Gabbs guided Spencer down to Mansfield Road and they turned left towards town. "What's going to happen when she gets out? She can't stay by herself can she?"

"She'll stay with us."

"That's a bit optimistic of you. Ain't it, Dad?"

He chuckled. "Optimistic, Gabbs? Can you even spell it?"

"Ha ha ha. Aren't you the funny one. But seriously. Della likes her own space. She'll want to go to her own house."

"Then we just need to convince her differently then, don't we."

"Are you going to marry her, Dad?"

He almost stumbled. "At one time she was my whole life," he said smoothly.

"But not now?"

"Let's just say we're two very different people, and I don't always know what's going on in her head."

"But isn't that a good thing, Dad. I read somewhere that the best time in a relationship is the beginning and I know you're enjoying yourself."

"Oh yeah. How?"

"You're nicer."

"Nicer?"

"Yeah, you laugh more and only shout at the stuff that really matters now. Not all that other stuff."

"You being the other stuff?"

"Of course, and don't forget you're more relaxed. I don't think you've ever gone for a walk like this, and you just love the house you're renting."

"True." First thing he'd do was landscape the garden if he bought it.

"So I think you should buy it," Gabbriella encouraged, unknowingly echoing his thoughts. "And we live up here and I can go to college."

They stopped in the street.

"You want to live up here?"

She nodded biting the corner of her bottom lip.

"I've enrolled in college, starting in January," she revealed.

"I see."

"Do you, Dad? Really? You can come up every weekend. I can live in the house with Isaac, and Della can always keep an eye on me."

"You've got it all worked out."

"Are you mad?"

"No."

"You sound mad."

"I'm not mad, Gabbs."

"Are you sure? 'Cause I really wasn't going to tell you until after Christmas."

"And that would make me feel better?"

"See, I told you you're mad," she said, pulling on his arm. "We need to cross."

"Where is this place?"

"Not far, another five minutes."

"Seems you and your brother get along."

"He's fab. A little weird sometimes, but yeah I like him."

"Weird how?" Spencer latched on.

"Like you, I guess. I told him about that car thingy."

"Car thingy?"

"Yeah, you know. That time me and my friends borrowed that car."

"Borrowed being the optimum word."

"He went all you on me. I swear if I'd closed my eyes it would have been you lecturing me." She stopped. "We're here."

They came face to face with a large three-storied Victorian house, four houses in from the end of a narrow street clogged with cars on either side.

"You wait here," Spencer ordered.

"I'm not staying here. It's cold."

"Gabbriella, please."

"Fine."

Spencer walked up the short pathway and knocked. The murmur of voices inside went mute.

A tall Rastafarian man answered the door and Spencer thought he looked vaguely familiar.

"I'm here to get Isaac."

"Isaac? The man said in a surprisingly cultured voice. "And who might you be?"

"I'm his—-I'm his—," Spencer couldn't say it. "I'm—"

The man looked him up and down with narrowed eyes then looked over at Gabbriella.

"Hey," he grinned. "You're the little princess sister."

Gabbriella smiled and nodded. She stomped her feet while blowing into her gloved hands to keep warm.

"Come in."

"You stay by the door," Spencer murmured to his daughter. "Leave the door open."

"Yes, Dad." Gabbriella looked at him as though she'd just sucked a lemon.

"Come this way," the cultured man invited.

Spencer followed him to the back of the house through a door that led to what turned out to be a huge modern kitchen. A group of seven men, including Isaac, were seated talking. Spencer recognised Ras Simeon, who stood up to greet him enthusiastically. He shook his hand and introduced him to everyone.

The room was filled with smoke, but instead of the acrid, pungent smell of weed, the air was surprisingly pleasant. The men were eating from large trays filled with various piles of food. It was like an Ethiopian restaurant Spencer had once visited.

Gabbriella entered the room and quickly accepted the invitation for them to stay for dinner.

★★★

"This is not up for discussion," Spencer warned as he listened keenly to the Sat Nav.

"What isn't?" Della asked.

"It would be better for all of us if you stay at my house."

"Okay."

143

Spencer stole a quick glance at her then turned to concentrate on the road again. He had been anticipating an epic battle, and had armed himself with a mental list of reasons she should stay with him. Hell, Gabbriella had even given him a point or two to convince Della to stay with them.

"You don't need to look so shocked," Della said with amusement.

"I thought you'd at least have something to say."

"What would be the point?" she sighed. "You've already made up your mind."

"Damn right." He grinned and touched her knee gently. "How are you feeling?"

"Just a little sore."

"Two puncture wounds to the abdomen will do that to a girl," he drawled dryly, still feeling that ripple of fright shoot through him.

"If you turn that thing off," she said, pointing to the Sat Nav, "and turn right, it'll be quicker."

"You sure?"

"This is my city," Della stated proudly. "Of course, I'm sure."

Spencer took the right at the four-way intersection and drove smoothly along an old tree-lined road with three-story houses on both sides. Some of the houses had been converted into offices. A huge modern-looking building called The Mary Potter Centre stuck out blatantly against the historic backdrop of the street.

He recognised the intersection and drove straight across it, knowing that the Forest Recreational Ground would be coming into view soon.

"Can you pull over for a sec?"

"Why? We're almost home, according to you."

"Yes, but before we get there I'd like to stretch my legs. I've been cooped up for days."

He wanted to argue but didn't want to mess with the amiable rapport they were having. Seeing a parking spot on the main road to his right, he parallel parked between two cars.

"I remember practising that with you."

"What?" Spencer asked, turning off the engine.

"Parking. You used to hit the sidewalk."

He grinned, remembering. They used to share the same driving instructor.

"It's a pavement," he said. "When in Rome..."

They laughed and he kissed her quickly as he helped her out of the flower-filled car. The entire backseat was covered with baskets of flowers from the night teams at her workplace, as well as from her day-shift colleagues. Della had always been popular, Spencer knew.

Della was holding her side as they walked slowly through three small pyramids of concrete and onto the grass. Two sets of football games were in progress. Plenty of runners were also making the most of the dry day.

Della and Spencer leaned against the wall that ran down one side of the huge park.

"Want an ice-cream?" he asked a moment later, seeing an ice-cream van parked near the playground.

She smiled. "I think he switches to mini doughnuts this time of year."

"Mini doughnuts?"

She looked at him cheekily. "Hot and covered with sugar. Divine."

"Mini doughnuts it is." With his hands in his pockets he walked off and Della watched him go. He'd been an absolute terror to the nurses and doctors, insisting they keep her in again last night. He'd only calmed down when they threatened to have him removed.

Della was trying to be brave and was putting up a pretty good front so no-one suspected how upset and frightened she really was. She'd been lucky. Lucky that the attacker's knife blade had been short. But every time she closed her eyes she felt the breath of Hoodie Boy on her face. She now knew what he'd been doing all that time when he was bent over her. He'd been cutting her hair.

For Della, her hair was more than just a style. It was her crown, proudly showing the world that she was a Rastafarian. Now she felt violated. She'd lost a piece of herself in that dirty alley and she was afraid.

"One bag of mini doughnuts and one plastic tray of every sauce the man had." Spencer held out a white paper bag.

"I'm just a surgery type of girl." Della picked up a doughnut and took a bite. It was hot and steaming and covered with an insane amount of sugar.

"I'm glad you're here," Della confessed.

"Thank you."

"Are you going to make this difficult for me?"

Spencer turned to look at her. She'd lost a few pounds, and her eyes had a lost haunted look about them. He wanted the feisty fire back.

"Yes."

She cut her eyes after him and raised her chin. He smiled, ready to provoke her natural defiance.

"I do like having you around," she said.

"Thank you."

"And I do appreciate all that you've done, especially these last few days. Knowing you were around looking out for Isaac took away a lot of the worry."

"No problem."

"How has he been, honestly?"

"All right. He's been staying with me and Gabbriella. His support worker, what was her name?"

"Casey."

"Yes, Casey. Cute little thing. She came round to see how you were doing. You know she likes him, don't you?" Spencer said.

"She does seem to be getting a little too close," Della replied, recalling the occasions she'd bumped into Casey at Isaac's gigs. She was a nice girl and Della liked her, but she would much prefer if Casey wasn't working with her son should they become romantically involved. "She's his support worker. She's not supposed to get too close."

Spencer frowned. That was not the response he'd been expecting. Was Della jealous?

"I heard you had a visitor the other night?" he asked, changing the subject.

Della smiled, remembering waking up in the middle of the night to see Fliss curled up on the single plastic chair.

"Hmm hmm. Fliss."

"You two close?" He knew very little about the girl.

"She's a good kid, just a little lost that's all."

"Her sales are good."

"You've been looking at our stats?"

Spencer shrugged. "Everyone's."

"Why?"

"Curious, really. I'll tell you this. That other night team is a little ahead in the Christmas incentive."

"That's only because I've been gone for a couple of days. We'll catch up when I get back."

"I doubt it."

"We're that far behind?"

"No. You're not going back," said Spencer.

"I'm only signed off for another week."

"And I'd like you to have a good rest. You may as well return in the New Year, if that's what you want."

Spencer was hiding something from her, Della told herself. But she was tired and unable to muster any enthusiasm for her job right now. Going back in the New Year was a blissful idea, but she'd make up her mind closer to the time.

"We'll see," she said, shivering.

"Come on. Let's get you inside." Spencer stood in front of her and buttoned her coat.

Della ate the last doughnut and dusted off her fingers. She crushed up the oil-stained paper bag and shoved it into her pocket. She took the hand Spencer held out and interlocked her fingers through his as they walked back to the car.

CAROLINE BELL FOSTER

## CHAPTER TWENTY

The coasters were wobbly, but that was it. Della couldn't find any other fault with Spencer's house. They'd arrived there by mid-afternoon, but Spencer didn't come inside. He simply unlocked the front door and told Della to make herself at home.

She felt like one of the women on that reality show Wife Swap looking through an unfamiliar home and trying to get an idea of who actually lived there by going from room to room and peering into the cupboards.

The place was cold and impersonal and as far from the house Spencer had rented in Nottingham—and even her own little terrace—as you could get. He'd really been slumming it in the Midlands.

Finally choosing a bedroom, Della curled up on a pale duvet to rest.

The heavy slam of a door later woke her up from an uncharacteristically deep sleep. She sat up, completely disorientated, and looked around the unfamiliar room.

"Della?" Spencer called out just as she unwound her legs and walked out to the landing.

"Here."

148

"Sorry I took so long," he said, walking towards the glass staircase he'd designed himself. "But once my staff knew I was in the building, everyone needed me urgently for something," he added with a lazy grin.

"That's fine. I fell asleep anyway." Della reached the second to last step and was fighting the urge to look back to see if she had left any finger marks on the chrome hand-rail. To Della, this house wasn't a home; it was an architectural delight, appreciated only from the fantasy of a glossy home and garden magazine. No-one really lived like this. It was no wonder Gabbriella preferred to spend her time out of it.

"Eat in or out?" Spencer asked as his eyes dipped low to sweep over her. Since the stabbing, Della had become a shadow of her normal self, and she looked as delicate as spun glass.

"Out."

Spencer's eyebrows shot up in surprise as he would have bet money on Della wanting to stay in, order a take-out, bury herself in a blanket and watch TV.

"Out it is then," he confirmed with a grin. "Let me grab a shower and change, and we'll go for a quick bite around the corner." He reached for her hand and squeezed it gently. He desperately wanted to see her feisty fire again. "Go freshen yourself up and I'll meet you here in half-an-hour." He ordered gently, kissing her quickly on the forehead before she could turn away.

***

So this was his place around the corner, Della thought in sudden panic. She wasn't dressed for the swanky hush and plush of muted black and gold elegance of the dimly lit room and almost said as much to Spencer. But what was the point, she asked herself, as she tipped up her chin, mustered a confident smile and handed her coat to the maître'd. There was no backing out now.

"What would you like?" Spencer asked. They were seated by a young good-looking waiter who looked vaguely familiar.

"I'm just going through the vegetarian options. There's a lot to choose from."

"Are you feeling, okay? Do you need me to translate for you?"

Della looked up from the menu and sighed inwardly with annoyance. He was seriously getting on her nerves, constantly asking if she was comfortable, or hungry, or if she needed something. She was beginning to feel smothered. "I think I can manage a little Italian, thank you," she replied with a tight smile.

"Fine." Spencer signalled for the waiter and watched with surprise as Della made her order in rapid Italian. Then he watched in growing disbelief as Della and the waiter launched into conversation that was too fast for him to follow. They both started laughing and the young waiter, completely forgetting himself, took Della's hand and kissed it. Della blushed like a schoolgirl. She hadn't laughed or looked this happy in days.

"What was that about?" Spencer asked, stiffly picking up his napkin and flicking it abruptly several times before putting it down beside his cutlery.

"Oh nothing," she replied, waving it off with a flutter of her hand.

Spencer didn't appreciate the gesture. "It didn't look like nothing."

Della sighed dramatically. "He said my Italian accent was perfect and that he loves reggae music."

"Why would he talk to you about reggae music?"

"It's my hair." Della picked up a lock and looked at it before resting it gently across her breast again. "And the assumption that comes with it."

Spencer looked at her, seeing her pretty, make-up free face, the dainty shell earrings she liked to wear, and the light blue headscarf that covered the choppy patch in her hair. She was wearing a bright orange floaty dress type thing with long slits at the sides, floaty trousers and black Doc Martins. She looked like a mixture of exotic cultures which was nice if she lived in the tropics, but he would rather she tone down on the whole mi is Rasta thing he thought.

"That's it?"

"And something about my order pleasing the chef, who's also his father," Della responded.

Spencer started to feel like a moody jackass. He was in Della's company and they were at his favourite restaurant. He should be bloody happy, he chided himself. Still, he wasn't pleased that it had taken a stranger to make her laugh.

Dinner was eaten in near silence. Spencer had given up on trying to draw Della into conversation. She was obviously uncomfortable and seemed desperate to be some place else, anywhere but here with him.

Their waiter Antonio, as he declared himself, swooped down on Della with the dessert menu and looked crestfallen when she declined, asking instead for a herbal tea.

There was a flutter of activity, then Antonio was back with a wooden box of different exotic teas. He and Della laughed as they talked in Italian.

Spencer didn't like it. She was never this happy and carefree with him.

"Let's go," he growled abruptly.

"But I haven't had my tea yet," she protested, trailing her fingers along the small packets being held out to her.

"I didn't bring you here to make a spectacle of yourself with the staff!" The words had flown out of Spencer's mouth.

"What?"

"You heard." He grabbed her by the arm and marched her to the foyer. He let her go when the young waiter produced a small white box containing a selection of teas and yet another larger box bearing a surprise from the chef. Spencer wanted to smash the swarmy bastard in the face.

★★★

"Spencer!" someone shouted behind them. "Spencer!"

Della stopped and turned, forcing Spencer to do the same. They were walking home from the restaurant.

A beautiful girl with extra-long model-perfect legs, swivelling hips and breeze-blown hair came towards them.

"Lovely to see you," she said to Spencer, and with sultry movements pressed herself against his chest. She ran her fingers up the lapel of his coat and around his neck to pull him down, planting kisses on both of his cheeks. Her micro dress inched up, showing the curve of her bottom.

Della, feeling like a third wheel, tried to pull away but Spencer wouldn't let her.

He stepped back, taking Della with him. "Joelle," he uttered finally.

"Where have you been?" Joelle asked lightly. "You completely missed our lunch date and no-one has seen you. Who's this?"

"This is Della."

Joelle looked Della up and down and then raised a questioning brow at Spencer.

Della just knew what she was thinking. What was Spencer Chandler-Wright doing with this dowdy dreadlocked woman. Story of my life, Della thought reliving that shadow of self consciousness that had blighted her teenaged self.

"Nice to meet you, Della," she said.

"And you too." Della shook the elegant hand that was extended to her.

"Have you eaten?" Joelle looked at the restaurant. "We can join up. I'm meeting my girlfriend here in a sec then we're going clubbing after."

"Sorry, we've just finished," Della replied. Spencer obviously wasn't in a hurry to answer. "Maybe another time?"

"That would be great," Joelle said with childish enthusiasm, much to Della's surprise. "Where's your phone?" Joelle quickly opened her miniscule bag.

Della didn't have a bag, so braving it out, reached inside her top and pulled out her phone from the strapping of her bra. Spencer looked horrified.

Joelle laughed. "I haven't seen that done since I left Martinique."

"You're from the Islands?" Della asked.

"I was Miss Martinique four years ago, and now I live here doing a bit of modelling. You're from Jamaica? You knew Spencer from before?"

"I've known Spencer practically all my life."

"Really?" Joelle moved closer to Della. "So you're not really together then?"

"Excuse us," Spencer interrupted sharply. "But it's cold and we've got to go."

He didn't understand women. He watched as they exchanged mobile numbers and promised to meet up before Della left London.

"I'd rather you didn't," Spencer said as he marched Della up the street a moment later.

"Didn't what?

"Get friendly with Joelle."

"Why? She seems nice."

"She's not like you."

"Meaning I'm just a short stupid fat woman without any sense?"

"That's not what I meant at all," he grumbled. "And stop putting words in my mouth, damn it. Joelle is a party animal. I don't want her influencing you."

Della laughed."Can you hear yourself? I'm not Gabbriella, you know, and I can make my own friends."

"But not with her."

"Have you slept with her?"

"Yes."

"Well, don't you think highly of yourself. Do you think you'll be the topic of conversation all the time? That we'll compare notes about you sexu—"

Spencer cut her off by swinging her around and kissing her brutally.

She pushed against his chest to fight him off, but he wrapped his arms tightly around her.

"What are you doing?" Della asked, wiping her mouth with the back of her hand a moment later.

"You're not in Joelle's league," Spencer began, then cursed as he realised how that sounded. "What I mean is—"

Della took two steps away from him.

"Don't bother to explain, Spencer. I know what you meant."

"Damn it, Della," he began again but the melodic sounds of Aswad interrupted him and he fished out his mobile. It was a rare thing when his eldest daughter rang him. "Hi baby girl," he said, answering the call.

He unlocked the front door, with the phone glued to his ear, and watched as Della went straight up the stairs without looking back.

# CHAPTER TWENTY-ONE

London was a mistake. She shouldn't have come, Della told herself. But Spencer had been super excited about showing her his home, and Gabbriella and Isaac were sold on the idea of having her recuperate away from her home.

There had been nothing but drama and arguments since Spencer had crow-barred himself back into her life and Della didn't like it. She strived for a life of tranquil simplicity, and at this point, to be honest, she wasn't sure she wanted a man in her life. She'd been without one for long and had managed just fine. Spencer seemed eager to recapture those sparkling years in Jamaica, and for a time Della had encouraged him. But now their relationship felt like a jigsaw puzzle; the picture was there, but some pieces were just too big to fit.

She and Spencer were different people and, if anything, last night had showed her just how different. He didn't understand her and was probably embarrassed by her. She was that jigsaw piece that didn't quite fit.

Spencer was prepared to grovel. He knew his behaviour last night was shameful, but he couldn't explain what had gotten over him. Seeing Della flirting with another man didn't sit well with him. He wasn't a jealous man. His wife had been an outrageous flirt and it never bothered him. But somehow seeing Della do it made his blood boil.

When they'd got home Della had ignored his offer to make her a drink and took herself to bed. It was now a day later and she still hadn't said a word to him. They were supposed to yell and shout. They weren't supposed to waste precious time with negative emotion. He'd brought her to London to recuperate and relax. He wanted to treat her to all those things she had to forgo as a single mother. He owed her.

* * *

Della was fuming. Seated next to her, Spencer was a ball of excitement as they waited for another model to come out in yet another outfit Della had no intention of wearing.

She eventually blanked it all out as the tall skinny model, who didn't look a day over fourteen, walked out in a slinky knee-length dress and sky-high heels. Spencer nodded his approval and the assistant at the side smiled in agreement and made a notation on her tablet.

Della tuned them out and scrolled through the messages on her phone. Isaac had not texted, but Gabbriella had sent a message saying they were okay and she was not to worry as they'd see her soon. Felicity had also sent a text asking about her condition and if they would see her at the Christmas party. Della had completely forgotten about the Christmas party and quickly texted back.

Spencer could feel his patience begin to crack. What the hell was the matter with Della? He was spending a fortune on her, and there she was playing with her phone. He wanted to snatch the damn thing out of her hands. She didn't even try to conceal her boredom. She never used to be like this.

An hour later, he took her to the salon Gabbriella used.

"Why am I here?" Della asked, glancing around the ultra-modern black-and-pink hair salon in trepidation as stylists and patrons eyed them curiously. A petite woman approached them, dressed in a bizarre type of military uniform, patent platform heels and purple spiky hair.

"My treat," Spencer whispered in Della's ear and, with a hand at the small of her back, pushed her forward. "I'll pick her up in three hours," he told the girl as he checked his watch. "Do what you can."

Della had long considered herself a strong woman who didn't need a man to validate her worth. But somehow Spencer's words took her back to a dark time years ago when her confidence had hit a seriously low point, thanks in no small part to his mother.

It was the start of the autumn school term, following a long summer of pool parties and shopping trips to Miami. Della had endured hours at the hairdresser's getting wefts of top quality hair sewn into her own tight curls.

Della remembered tossing her new hair this way and that and winding down the car window so the summer breeze could dive through it. She'd loved it and after a quick shower she'd put on her new denim shorts that turned over at the cuff, a red bra top and to cover it, a little black jacket with shoulder pads. Red lipstick, gold anchor earrings, white socks and black boots completed the look. She could have been the fourth member of Salt & Pepa, their favourite rap band back then, and she was dying to show Spencer her new look.

She opened the heavy ornate gate to the Chandler-Wright residence and played with their massive rottweilers as she bounced up the winding driveway. She could hear talking on their balcony and she bounded into the house with breathless excitement.

The whole family was there. Mr Chandler-Wright smoking a fat cigar, as he always did after dinner. Mrs. Chandler-Wright was saying something to Jeremy, and Spencer had his back to her. The Chandler-Wrights were the only people Della knew who used the word maids to refer to their household helpers, who wore black and white uniforms. A pair of them were standing to the side.

Mrs. Chandler-Wright had stopped talking, mid-sentence, and stared at Della. "Well, if it isn't Little Miss-Can't-Be," she drawled, raising an eyebrow in disdain. Jeremy and the staff snickered.

Spencer turned around sharply. Mr. Chandler-Wright switched the cigar from one side of his mouth to the other in amusement.

"You can buy your hair and bleach your skin, sweetie," she continued. "But you will never be one of us."

Della could still feel the sting of those words on her skin and hear their laughter as she ran out of the house. Spencer had called out to her, but she had sped across their lawn, tripping over the dogs and scratching her boots. Blinded by tears, she'd scrambled over the fence and into her own house.

Utterly humiliated, Della cut off the new hair and got one of her helpers to cut the stitching from what was left of the wefts with a razor. She hadn't worn hair extensions since.

Back at the salon, Della watched wretchedly as Spencer made his exit and climbed into his car. She felt raw and ugly.

The stylist tried to hide it, but Della could tell she really didn't know what to do.

"Shall I wash it?" she asked, looking at Della's hair as though it was Medusa's very own mane.

"Do you know how?" Della replied, trying to soften her sarcasm with a small smile.

"Well, not really," said the stylist with a shrug. Laughter erupted behind them.

Della slumped into the chair the girl had shown her to. "Do whatever," she whispered and closed her eyes.

She kept her eyes closed as the girl plucked her eyebrows and later sprayed make-up on her face. She kept them closed as the girl unwound her headscarf and she kept them closed when she heard the buzz of electric hair clippers close to her ear.

* * *

As instructed via text, Della told the bouncer her name and watched with amusement as he looked at a clipboard, checked her name off and then offered the crook of his arm. He escorted her down a long corridor lit by the glow of six huge fish-tanks on either side. Not a single fish was in sight.

It wasn't the kind of atmosphere Joelle had promised. Della was expecting a night with Carroll Thompson, JC Lodge and other lover's rock artists. Instead, she was hit in the face by heavy bass and the piercing sound of a wailing cat as the bouncer opened the metal door at the end of the corridor.

Another bouncer invited her over to the VIP section. Searching for Joelle, Della pushed her way through the crowd.

"Della!"

Della found herself wrapped in a tight embrace and then held off at arm's length.

"You look amazing. Love the hair." Joelle reached up and touched what was left of Della's dreadlocks. The stylist had cut them to what she said was a more reasonable length. They now hung just above her shoulders, swept over to one side in what the stylist had declared was the latest fashion to show off the shaved side of her head.

Della had been horrified when she'd finally opened her eyes and looked at herself. She blamed herself. She'd sat in numb disbelief for a long while, as everyone waited to see her reaction. She'd eventually smiled and said the right things. Yes, her new eyebrows were amazing, and the new haircut shone with its bleached blonde ends.

Spencer came to pick her up and said not a single word when he saw her new look. The silence remained unbroken till they got home and he asked if she was happy with the change. She said yes. He'd looked at her searchingly, shook his head and left the room. Della sat at the kitchen table and cried.

Della had been splashing cold water on her swollen eyes when Joelle called and invited her out. And here she was, out enjoying herself.

"What would you like to drink?" Joelle asked close to her ear. The music was too loud for normal conversation.

"A cranberry juice please."

"What?" Joelle's eyes widened. "Just cranberry?"

Della nodded. "I don't drink alcohol," she confessed.

Joelle turned to one of the adoring men nearby and whispered in his ear then turned back to Della.

"Love the dress," Joelle complimented as Della tugged at the hem of her lacy, form-fitting red dress. "Where's Spencer, by the way?"

"I don't really know," Della admitted. She hadn't seen him since he'd walked out of the kitchen.

"He doesn't know you're out with me?" Joelle looked a little peeved.

"No. Sorry."

"Hmm."

Joelle's male friend came back with two glasses of heavily iced cranberry juice. "Here." Joelle handed one to Della. "To a good night out!" She touched her glass to Della's with a clunk. "Woo hoo!"

She laughed as she introduced Della to the group.

## CHAPTER TWENTY-TWO

Della was having a good time. The music wasn't bad and the conversation was loud and lively. She hadn't laughed so much in years and was really enjoying herself with Rowan, the attentive rugby player who kept telling her how beautiful she was. She even danced in her high heels, basking in the heavy sound of the music as it vibrated through her body, bringing her to life.

Della hadn't danced in years and found herself sashaying on the dance floor, her arms flung over her head as Rowan gyrated his pelvis into hers. He spun her around in dizzying speeds as the music got faster.

"I've got to go to the ladies'," Della told Rowan breathlessly, leaning heavily into him. He looked like a hulking bull, all thick neck and muscles. With a hand brushing the underside of her breasts, she let him guide her to the bathroom and open the door for her.

Della didn't know why she was so unsteady on her feet. Must be the heels, she thought, as she walked carefully across the black and white chequered floor, skipping the large white ones to step only on the black.

She lurched into a stall, lifted her dress high, forgetting it was so short and laughed out loud as she almost took the whole thing off over her head.

Then she had difficulty getting the tissue from the dispenser as it kept going round and round and she kept missing the end until a long length of the stuff floated to the floor and she ripped it off, put it in the toilet and tried again. This went on for several minutes as Della couldn't get her fingers to do what she wanted them to do.

She eventually got up and wobbled over to the row of sinks, counting five pink sinks in all. She wanted to use the fourth one.

"You can use this one love," a girl told her, but Della shook her head. She wanted the fourth sink. "Suit yourself." The girl shrugged and went back to re-gluing her fake eyelash.

As she waited, Della stared at a woman in the full length mirror. She was wearing a dress one had to be super confident to wear. It plunged down low and rode up high. She was very pretty, her make-up flawless, her eyebrows nicely arched and framing huge brown eyes that looked glazed if a little lost.

Della turned to ask the woman if she was okay but she had disappeared. She turned back and the woman was there.

Della swayed and grabbed the counter as a veil of suffocating heat covered her.

"I've got to go," Della told Joelle as she walked unsteadily from the ladies' room. She was battling the first waves of nausea that was crawling up her throat.

"It's still early Della and I think Rowan there will be disappointed," Joelle said, looking at the rugby player Della had been dancing with. He was busy chatting up a voluptuous redhead and hadn't noticed them.

"I doubt it," Della stated. "What was in my drinks, Joelle?"

Joelle shrugged but smiled too widely for Della's liking. "Vodka," she admitted without apology. "You were looking a bit stressed when you got here so I thought it would loosen you up a bit."

"But I told you I don't drink."

"So?" Joelle's mouth flattened into a tight ugly line.

"This wasn't about me. Was it, Joelle?" Della asked not sure if the alcohol was playing with her mind, as she saw dark cracks of ugliness appearing beneath Joelle's skin.

"No hard feelings, Della." Joelle patted Della on the head. "You're nice enough but this was about Spencer."

Della nodded stiffly and walked away, concentrating on taking step after step but helplessly bumping into the heaving bodies dancing. Someone stepped on her foot, the flimsy straps on her shoes offered little protection as she cried out and stumbled against a tall blonde man who spun around, his ready apology dying on his lips as he gaped at her.

"Della?"

Della looked up through the blur of tears and pain. "Mac?" It was surreal seeing her work colleague there.

"Please," she whispered. "Take me away from here."

***

"What the hell did you do?" Spencer charged at Mackenzie as soon as he walked into the flat.

"Don't shout. It isn't his fault," Della whispered as she sat curled up with a mug of hot tea in her hand and a blanket around her shoulders.

"Where the hell have you been? I didn't even know you'd gone out, and then I get a phone call like this? You've been out drinking!"

"I didn't purposefully go out drinking," Della shot back, putting her cup down and uncurling her legs. "Listen, this is Mac's place and I've intruded long enough. We can do this later."

Spencer pulled himself together. He'd been out of his mind with worry since Mackenzie had rung him. He'd thought Della was upstairs sulking and couldn't believe she'd gone out clubbing without him knowing. She'd even gotten so drunk she blacked out. Thankfully Mackenzie had had the forethought to ring him.

"Listen." Spencer turned to the young man who was hovering self-

163

consciously by the open plan kitchen. "Thank you for looking after her."

Mackenzie nodded. "You going to be all right, Della?"

"Yes. Thank you, sweetheart." She shrugged out of the blanket and turned to fold it.

"You went out dressed like that!" Spencer roared.

Della looked down at herself. "You bought it."

"When we get home I'm going to burn it," Spencer muttered darkly. He took off his coat and dropped it heavily over her shoulders. "Let's go." He turned to Mackenzie, extending his hand. "Thanks for looking after her. As you can see, she doesn't seem to have a clue."

"It's all right mate," Mackenzie replied and then turned to Della. "You didn't see me and I didn't see you." He tapped the side of his nose.

Della went over hugged him hard and kissed him on the cheek.

"Thank you," she whispered. She then went for her shoes and grimaced as she put them on.

"For the love of God," Spencer sighed. Kneeling down, he swiftly removed her shoes and picked her up. He waited for Mackenzie to open the door then carried her out to the car.

On the ride home Spencer was so incensed he could barely contain his rage. Della, meanwhile, was fast asleep, her head wobbling against the window as Spencer drove along the quiet London street.

What was she thinking? Della was never impulsive like this and she never drank. As far as Spencer knew, Rastafarians didn't drink. What was going on in her head that she would do what she did tonight? He gripped the steering wheel as he overtook a slow-moving milk float. The stabbing had changed her, Spencer concluded. She hadn't been herself since.

Once home, he undressed her and put her to bed. Then, with the red dress crumpled in one tight fist and her shoes in his other hand, he walked outside and dropped the items into the galvanised incinerator at the bottom of the back garden and set them ablaze.

## CHAPTER TWENTY-THREE

Della had never felt so sick in her life. It was a funny kind of sickness not in any one part of her body. If this was what a hangover felt like, she failed to see why people would intentionally put themselves through it every weekend.

She vaguely remembered Spencer stripping off her clothes and putting her to bed, his eyes cold and his mouth pressed into a tight disapproving line.

What had she done? How could Joelle lace her drinks like that and think it was ok? How could some people be so immoral and manipulative?

Della remembered Joelle and her friends putting glass after glass into her hands. And she drank them all, thinking she was simply quenching her thirst from all the dancing. It was an awful night, and now she had to get out of bed and face the world. Thank goodness Isaac and Gabbriella weren't here to witness her shame.

Della reluctantly opened her eyes. The curtains were drawn. She reached for her phone to see the time. It wasn't there.

With a soft groan she sat up and pressed her fingers into her temples. Her head was swimming. She suddenly noticed Spencer seated in a chair he must have brought into the room, watching her silently in the shadows.

"Drink that glass of water and take the tablets before you get out of bed," he advised quietly. "You'll feel better in a bit."

A glass, a blister of panadol and a jug of water sat on the mirrored bedside table.

"What time is it?" Della rubbed her hands over her face and flipped her hair from her eyes. Her tongue felt thick and furry.

"It's late." Spencer poured her a glass of water and held it out to her. "Drink."

"Thank you."

As she finished, he poured her another one. "You'll feel better once you've hydrated yourself."

She looked at him from under her lashes. He was wearing dark jeans a white t-shirt with a thin navy jumper over it. His eyes were red. His hair was a mess.

"Are you going to shout?" she asked softly. He looked more resigned than angry, which made Della feel even worse.

"What would be the point?"

"You're making me feel guilty, just sitting there looking at me. I know you want to shout."

"You don't know anything." Spencer stood up and walked to the door. "Go and freshen up, and I'll make you something to eat."

"I can't face food right now," said Della.

"I'll see you in the kitchen."

"Fine." She flipped the covers open only to flip them quickly over herself again, as she realised she was naked. Spencer had a small smirk on his face.

"I undressed you."

"Thank you."

They stared at each other. They were about to have an almighty row. They could feel it coming. But neither of them wanted to start it.

## CHAPTER TWENTY-FOUR

Della felt much better after showering and brushing her teeth. She'd managed to do that without looking in the mirror. The wardrobe full of new clothes that had been there yesterday were gone and Della assumed Spencer had moved her room around. If he thought she was going to be sleeping with him he had another think coming. She fumed as she pulled on her leggings and a fleecy green jumper that reached her knees. She ran her hands along the fabric, wishing she were back in Nottingham in her own comfy house with her cat.

"Toast," Spencer said, as Della entered the kitchen and sat at the round glass table. "Eat."

"Will you stop ordering me about."

He ignored her and put a plate of hot buttery toast down in front of her as though she hadn't spoken.

"Coffee or mint?"

"I'll get it."

"Sit down!"

Della stood up and faced him with her hands on her hips. "Get it out, Spencer, as I'm not going to be treated like a child, or I'm leaving."

"All right," he breathed, mirroring her stance and placing his own hands on his hips as he faced her. "Why would you disrespect me and leave my house as you did?"

"I didn't think about it."

"So I don't even warrant the courtesy of letting me know you were going out even though you are a guest in my home and we are lovers?"

"We are not lovers, and you went off in a sulk."

"We are lovers, but it's not even about that. Why would you go out with Joelle?"

"She asked."

"You don't even know her!"

"She sounded genuine on the phone."

"She's a bitch."

"A bitch you thought good enough to sleep with!"

"Sexual release, Della. That's all it was. My emotions were never involved with her."

"Well how wonderful for you to be able to separate your emotions like that! She obviously wanted more."

"We're not talking about me right now. This is about you dressing like a slut and getting drunk just to get back at me!"

"You bought the dress, Spencer, and many others just like it."

"I burnt it."

"I beg your pardon?"

"I burnt it along with the shoes."

"How dare you!"

"It doesn't matter now," he shrugged. "I sent the clothes back, too."

"What?"

"I sent them back to the store."

She sat down and held her head in her hands.

"What do you want from me, Spencer?"

"It's not about what I want, Della. It's you putting yourself at risk like that with people you don't know! Jesus Christ," he bellowed. "I've had this conversation with my daughters. I didn't expect to be having it with you, too!"

She jumped up quickly. "I've been looking after myself for years. I knew what I was doing!"

"Oh really," he scoffed. "You bought the alcohol?"

"Well, no."

"So you didn't know what you were doing," he said grimly. "Did you know your friend Mackenzie was going to be there?

"No, but—"

"But nothing. If he hadn't been there, God only knows what could have happened to you. And you say you can look after yourself."

"I didn't know Joelle had put vodka in my juice," Della replied. "You know I don't drink."

"I don't know anything about you anymore, Della. The woman I thought I knew wouldn't have behaved the way she did."

"Now you hold on!" Della really wanted to swear at him, but had already let herself down last night and wasn't about to add to it. "You're not being fair!"

"I don't know what's going on with you anymore." Spencer's shoulders slumped as though he'd been propping her up his entire life but had now given up.

The kitchen table was between them, and they stared at each other as three decades of silent hurt came pouring to the surface like battery acid.

"I've let you into my life when I didn't even know you!" Della raged at him.

"Let me!" Spencer straightened again not believing what he had just heard.

"Yes, let you. I was perfectly all right. Just me and Isaac."

"You buried yourself in England and smothered him so much he can barely take care of himself."

"That's not true!"

"He's an adult but you treat him like a little kid."

"He has a disability."

"I'm not disputing that, but you're not letting him think for himself or do anything for himself. You've ensured he can't make it without you. Relying on you totally."

"That's not true," Della repeated, struggling to hold back the tears. "I'm his mother. I'm all he has."

"But not anymore," Spencer said firmly.

"I'm his mother. It's my job to make his life easier."

"And I'm his father, and I'm telling you to let go of that choke hold you have around the poor boy's neck. Jesus Christ, Della!" Spencer threw his arms up in the air in frustration.

"Don't you judge me."

"Why not? You've been judging me. Making me believe the boy smokes weed when in fact he suffers from light sensitivity!"

"I —" Della was suddenly struck with guilt.

"You were happy to let me believe the worse so you could feel better about yourself."

"That's not true," Della said softly.

"Oh yeah, it is, my love," said Spencer, his tongue dripping with sarcasm. "You would let me believe my son was a drug addict, and shall I tell you why? It was never about how we were in Jamaica or even here. This is about you and your own feelings. You've never known who you are."

"I have."

"No, Della. I know you. I've always known you better than you know yourself. I might not have seen you in years, but I know how you think. You're always the victim and in some weird way happy to let me flounder and think the worse of Isaac. How could you do that?"

Della looked at him, shocked into silence. She didn't know what to say but she could feel a heavy darkness creep like tar up from the floor and into her body. Was it evil? Was she an evil person? Was this darkness always with her as she tried, but always failing, to find her purpose in life?

"And since when have you been so stupid, totally spineless and downright gullible?" he accused viciously.

She snapped out of her own thoughts at his mean words. "How dare you say that!"

"Because it's true. Ever since the incident you've not been yourself."

"I was stabbed, Spencer. You can say it."

"Stabbed!" He closed his eyes, reliving her horror and his own for one terrible second."You survived, Della." He reached for her hands. "You're here but you've been moping around, neglecting—"

"I have not been neglecting anyone! I was stabbed. Don't you think I need a little time to get over that?" Her eyes were filled with tears. "I was violently attacked because I'm different. He cut off my dreads!"

"And you let some silly hairdresser butcher the rest!" Spencer replied angrily. "They took years to reach that length. How could you let her do that? They were a symbol of your strength!"

"She just finished what that boy had started!" Della charged, pulling her hands violently away and stalking to the other side of the room. "And it's what you wanted."

"I never told you that! Have I ever interfered with your beliefs? Have I ever asked you to change? Well, have I?

She looked at him, the tears tipping onto her face. "No, but I know you hate it."

"Don't make assumptions, Della," he said quietly, trying to rein in his anger. "This is on you."

They looked at each other across the room, both silently feeling the emotion pulsating around them. It was too much for Della. She could feel the darkness seeping into her bones weighing her down.

"Where has my fiery and proud Rasta woman gone?" Spencer asked eventually, but before she could answer he slammed his mouth over hers and kissed her with all he was worth.

Della felt the kitchen counter at her back and made a sound deep in her throat when Spencer lifted her up to sit on the surface.

His large hands moved over her in a frenzy, going beneath her jumper to sweep up and cup her breasts.

Della tipped her head back as Spencer moved along her face,

dotting tiny kisses along her jawline to nip at her ear.

"Why do I let you do this to me?" he whimpered as he moved up to suck gently on her bottom lip.

"What?"

"Treat me like this?"

"I don't understand."

His thumbs rubbed to and fro over her painfully aching nipples and she thrust her chest against his warm hands.

"Blow hot and cold."

"I don't."

"You do."

She leaned back to see his face. "I do not blow hot and cold."

Spencer pulled her forward again and rested his forehead against hers. They were both breathing heavily.

"You tell me to keep my distance, yet you're here in my home knowing how I feel about you," he said. "You tell me you don't want me in your bed, then give me access to your body. You're a Rastafarian but you let someone cut off your beautiful hair." He cupped her head with his large hands and gently brushed her cheeks with his thumbs. "You don't know what you want, Della."

He kissed her gently, stepped back and looked at her. "You need to figure out who you are so you can continue with your journey. I want to walk it with you but you're like a map with no road signs and I'll be damned if I let you blindly lead the way. You have to do this one on your own."

He exited the room, leaving Della surrounded by guilt and silence.

# CHAPTER TWENTY-FIVE

The house was quiet. Della had gone back to bed with the weight of guilt heavy on her chest. And hours later it was still there.

Getting out of bed, she went into the adjoining bathroom, switched on the light, closed the door with a soft thud and finally looked at herself in the large bevelled mirror.

She didn't know herself like this. Her face was scrubbed clean, but dark globs of mascara clung to her lashes. Her once lovely hair was now chopped to make her look like a manufactured pop star instead of the earthy woman she really was.

Who was she now any way? She reached up and touched the shaved patch of scalp. Where had her true self gone?

Large fat tears rolled down her face and dripped onto the naked slopes of her breasts. She didn't recognize the person staring back at her. She locked her arms around her waist and cried.

Why did she let them do this to her? Why hadn't she fought back in the alleyway when she was being attacked? She'd let the hairdresser cover her face with artificial products, concealing the woman she was. She'd worn that dress Spencer had bought. She didn't know herself like this. Her soul was ashamed.

Opening the bottom drawer, she picked up a pair of scissors with one hand and a ropey strand of hair with the other. She cut it. She picked up another strand and yet another, ignoring the tears rolling down her cheeks. When all the hair was gone she looked at herself. It was like she was in a trance, the air still and quiet and stifling.

"What are you doing!" Spencer gasped from the doorway. He'd been working in his office downstairs and had come up to check on her. Hearing a noise from the bathroom, he'd followed the sound.

He wrestled the shaver from Della's cold fingers and threw it to the ground. It fell and vibrated into a corner, where it continued to buzz against the tiles. Spencer ignored it. "What have you done?"

Della didn't answer. She seemed dazed, her eyes vacant and large. He grasped her face and tipped her head up to inspect her closely. The pupils in her dark eyes were large and dilated, her skin cold and clammy.

She was clearly in shock.

Locks of her hair covered the bathroom floor. She'd cut off all her dreadlocks and had started using the shaver to remove the islands of tight curls left on her scalp.

She was sobbing. The deep gut-wrenching sounds pierced through Spencer's heart. He grabbed a towel and gently wound it around her. He then picked her up and lay with her on the bed to hold her close.

She sobbed into his chest, and he could hear her saying, 'My hair, my hair' over and over again between her hiccuping gasps.

When she finally went to sleep Spencer tip-toed out of the room, made a phone call he really didn't want to make and returned with a chair so he could watch over her as she slept.

## CHAPTER TWENTY-SIX

It was never going to be an easy conversation.

Standing beside the closed door in the guest bedroom recently vacated by Della, Spencer was trying to explain her absence to a ruffled Isaac, who was seated at the edge of the bed, staring blankly at the wall.

"Ras Simeon thought it best she go to a quiet place to rest," Spencer explained, realising he and his son had never shared a serious conversation before.

"This place was supposed to be her place to rest."

"I know, but a few things happened and she got upset."

"What things?" Isaac finally looked at him, but Spencer would have preferred a vacant stare instead of the blaze of mistrust and accusation that was now levelled at him. "If you hurt my mother I'm going to—"

"I would never hurt your mother," Spencer said heatedly, "and you know that too!" He scrubbed his hands over his face.

"You need to understand," he implored, moving away from the door to sit in the small single chair nearest to Isaac. "There was a time when all I wanted was to marry her. I loved her, and she is still very special to me."

Isaac glared at him from behind the blue tint of his glasses. Spencer returned the stare and waited. It mattered that Isaac believed him and the small nod of acceptance Isaac eventually gave him was a relief.

"The attack back in Nottingham," Spencer began again grimly when Isaac said nothing, "affected her more than she wanted us to know." He cleared his throat, aware that he wasn't explaining things properly. "She doesn't look like she used to."

"What?"Isaac shifted closer, leaning his head to one side.

"She cut her hair off."

"Her dreads?"

Spencer nodded.

"To what end?" Isaac asked, now leaning back as though distancing himself from something he didn't understand.

"I don't know. She was upset and confused an—"

"Confused about being a Rasta woman?"

Spencer shrugged. "I really don't know and only she can answer that. Ras Simeon came and took her away."

"Where?"

"Somewhere in Derbyshire."

"She went there before, that time when that man slapped her and—"

"What man?" Spencer asked.

"Some man I had to smash his face in before I found peace, and Rasta became my heart."

"What man?"

"Her boyfriend from when I was eleven and three months. He kept ordering me about and wanting to spend the night. Mum didn't like it and she told him to leave. He hit her and I hit him."

"But you were very young."

"She's my mother. She's royal."

"I'm glad you were there for her."

Isaac nodded and then glanced around the room as though

committing it to memory.

"I'll take a train back."Isaac got up and reached for his backpack on the floor beside the bed.

"No!" Spencer grabbed the bag and moved swiftly to stand in front of the bedroom door. "You can stay."

"But—"

"I want you to stay," Spencer said firmly.

"Why?"

Spencer was thrown by the question. "I promised your mother I'd look after you."

"I can take care of myself."

"I know you can," Spencer said, smiling. "But I really want you to stay and get to know you and for you to get to know us a little better too."

"You mean Nicole and Jesse? My sisters?"

"Yes. You can meet Nicole."

"I've already met her."

"When?"

"Skype. Lil' sis hooked us up."

Spencer hadn't seen Nicole in months. He needed to sort this all out. He wanted his family back and everything in order by the time Della came home. Ras Simeon had said at least a month. Thirty days to change his life.

"Will you stay?"

Isaac reached for his backpack and placed it on the floor beside the bed.

***

"Dad?"

Surging forward in his seat, Spencer gripped his mobile phone as a million unpleasant scenarios thundered rapidly through his mind. He steeled himself as he said, "What is it, Gabbriella?"

"I can't find Isaac."

He sighed, relieved, when he didn't hear the words dead, accident or police. "What do you mean? I thought you were doing some shopping?"

"We did, but it was so crowded. People everywhere. And then I just sorta lost him."

"Have you rung him?"

"'Course. No signal and I daren't move."

Spencer snapped his laptop shut, picked up his keys and walked to the coat stand. "How long ago?"

"An hour or so."

"An hour!"

"I thought I could find him!"Gabbriella replied. Spencer heard the distress in her voice.

"Where are you now?"He put on his heavy coat and headed for the elevator.

"In Harrods."

Spencer closed his eyes. "I'm coming. Tell a member of staff what happened and stay on the floor you lost him on."

"Yes, Dad."

"Which floor?"

"Third."

"Department?"

"Tech."

"I'm going in the lift now," he told her. "Stay where you are."

"Yes, Dad."

Spencer ended the call and leaned tiredly against the panelled wall as the lift sailed smoothly down twelve floors to the car park. He stepped out and signalled the driver he rarely made use of.

"Sir?"

"Harrods, please."

"Yes, sir."

Spencer settled into the back seat of the luxury car and closed his eyes as the driver navigated through the heavy, frustrating traffic. It had been four days since Della had left and two days since Gabbriella and Isaac had been in London.

He'd promised Della he would look after Isaac. Those were his last words to her as she clung to his hand, as Ras Simeon waited in the car ready to take her to the sanctuary in Derbyshire. It was a place they used, Ras Simeon said, when they needed time alone, to reconnect with their inner selves and meditate. Della had been there once before. But this time she didn't want to go, and it was only after extracting that promise from him that she finally relented. Della trusted him enough to look after Isaac, and he didn't intend to let her down.

Spying Harrods in the distance, Spencer gave the driver some instructions and exited the vehicle to fight his way through the crowds. It was bad. What happened to everyone shopping online and ordering luxury hampers, he wondered. He was surrounded by women laden with large bags. A pushchair knocked against his ankles. Perfume was squirted mere centimetres from his face. No wonder Gabbs had lost her brother. The place was a cattle market with sleigh bells playing in the background!

"Daddy!" Gabbriella yelled, as Spencer fought his way out of the lift and walked towards his daughter.

Tears had clearly smeared her mascara and she'd eaten her lipstick off.

"Anything?" Spencer asked.

She looked down at her phone. "I can't get a signal in here, but that man over there wants to talk to you." Tucking her hand safely in his, she led him over to a large MI5-type looking security guard who was talking into the white brightness of his shirt cuff.

"Roberts." The man introduced himself with a firm handshake. "We've got him leaving the store," he told Spencer in a no-nonsense, I'm-in-charge-of-the-field kind of way. "We caught him going to the tube station."

Spencer paled, picturing Isaac trying to navigate the underground.

"But he changed his mind and is now heading—hold on a minute." The guard tipped his head to one side as he listened to his earpiece before talking into his cuff again. "Looks like he might be heading to Hyde Park," he told Spencer.

Spencer thanked him, grabbed Gabbriella and marched from the store.

"What's happening, Dad?"

"I've got the driver circling outside. What's Isaac wearing?"

Gabbriella gave him a description, which he passed on to the driver.

"We'll grab a taxi."

"Might be faster to walk, Dad," Gabbriella said as they exited the building. They were greeted by a river of bumper-to-bumper cars.

"You're right. Come on."

Five minutes later Spencer's mobile rang and the driver put Isaac on the phone.

"You okay?" Spencer asked.

"Yeah."

"Stay right there. We're coming, okay?"

"Yeah."

Spencer would have been surprised if Isaac had said any thing else.

Gabbriella rushed into her brother's arms as soon as she saw him and started crying. Spencer watched with a lump in his throat as his two children clung to each other. Isaac then tucked his sister under his arm and turned to him.

"You okay, son?" Spencer took note of Isaac's flushed cheeks.

Isaac dipped his head and lowered his woolly hat onto his forehead before looking up again. A shy smile tugged at the corner of his mouth.

"Come on, let's get out of here." Spencer returned the smile, putting an arm around Isaac's shoulders as they walked towards the waiting car.

## CHAPTER TWENTY-SEVEN

"Everything all right?" Spencer asked, turning on the light as he stepped into the kitchen later that night.

After the incident earlier in the day, Spencer ensured all their telephone numbers and home and work addresses were put in Isaac's phone. He got Isaac to teach him the symbols he and Della used when all was not okay.

Spencer felt guilty that he'd forgotten about the dyspraxia because Isaac had functioned so well in Nottingham. But then, he now realised, Della usually ensured that Isaac didn't deviate from his routine at all. Spencer did his best to remember all the alarms and rules that got Isaac through his day. He decided that what Isaac really needed was a holiday routine they all could follow. So he had them sit down and painstakingly schedule what they would be doing over the next few days.

Isaac was in the kitchen with the fridge door partially open. He was seated at the table doing something to his leg.

"Sorry." Spencer apologised quickly and moved to turn off the harsh overhead light when Isaac covered his eyes with his hand.

Isaac nodded his thanks.

"What are you doing?" Spencer asked. They were communicating a lot better these days, but it always took a few minutes for them to warm up. Isaac never ever initiated a conversation.

"Wiping this up," Isaac said without lifting his head.

Spencer bent down to see what 'this' was. "When did you do that?" Spencer was shocked to see a deep gash on his son's shin and a trickle of blood.

"It's nothing."

"Like hell." Spencer opened the fridge door wider so that they were both bathed in a bright orange glow. "Straighten your leg out," he ordered. The gash was horizontal, short and deep. There were similar ones in the same area.

"How did this happen?" Spencer asked. He stood up and searched the overhead cupboards for the first-aid box.

"Tripped."

"Where?" Spencer saw Isaac shrug from the corner of his eye. "Where?" he asked again, finding the green plastic box and opening it on the counter.

"The stairs," Isaac said with obvious reluctance.

"You tripped on the stairs?"

Isaac shrugged again. "I always do."

Spencer nodded, remembering a conversation he'd had with Gabbriella about him tripping over things and his problems with perception. Not all dyspraxics struggled in that way, but Isaac did.

"I guess my glass staircase did the damage."

Isaac nodded and held out his hand for the packet of antiseptic wipes Spencer was holding.

"I'll do it," Spencer said without thinking, crouching on the floor.

Their eyes locked and it hit him. Right then. That sharp electrical zap through his heart when he'd first held Nicole, then Jesse, then Gabbriella. A zapping that coincided with tears, hugs and Hello Kitty plasters on skimmed knees. A zap of paternal instinct and hard-to-explain feelings.

The nod Isaac gave him was brief.

Spencer concentrated on stilling the slight tremble in his hands, as he wiped the cut. He pressed down on the wound to stop the bleeding and then rapidly shook the small can of spray plaster he'd found, took off the lid and prayed into the gash.

"I don't think you need stitches," he joked a moment later. "The other one?" He indicated Isaac's other leg.

"That one is all right."

"Sure?"

"Yeah. I always miss the third step," Isaac confessed quietly.

There was an uneasy silence while Spencer washed his hands and put away the first-aid box.

"I keep it in here," he said as he closed the cupboard door. Isaac would probably need to make use of the box. "Do you want a drink or something?"

Spencer almost smiled when he saw Isaac eyeing the door longingly, obviously ready to bolt.

"Hot chocolate? Milk?" he asked casually.

"Chocolate, please," Isaac said.

Spencer went about making the drink, deciding to heat the milk in a saucepan instead of the microwave and then went hunting for the nutmeg grater. Della always made hot chocolate with nutmeg.

"Gabbs told me about your driving lessons."

"Yeah."

"Yeah. How about I take you out sometime?" Spencer offered, turning around to lean against the counter.

A blaze of excitement lit up Isaac's eyes before he said, "It's all right."

"Not a problem. Do you want to know a secret?" Spencer asked, pausing to select the largest mugs. Isaac nodded, intrigued. "Your mother thinks she passed her driving test before me." Spencer stirred in the cocoa powder. "But she didn't," he said as he placed the mugs on the table. "I just let her think that." He pulled out a chair and sat down. "She always liked to win, you see."

Isaac smiled and Spencer relaxed into his seat as a warm silence filled the room.

\*\*\*

"Left left left!" Spencer grabbed the steering wheel and yanked it towards him. "What the hell was that?" he yelled.

"Sorry."

"Sorry! You were about to go down a one-way street! Didn't you see the sign?"

"I said sorry."

Spencer drew in a deep shuddering breath. This should have been a bonding exercise, something for the two of them to do together. But it was a disaster. An absolute bloody disaster.

"Pull over there," Spencer snapped, pointing to a parking space between two cars. He was left gob-smacked, his mouth hanging open, when Isaac slid the BMW into the narrow spot in two seconds flat.

Spencer sat there in stunned disbelief that Isaac had smoothly parked the car between a brand new Range Rover and a snazzy Z4 with inches to spare. If he hadn't just witnessed it he wouldn't have believed it. It just wasn't possible.

Then he turned to Isaac and grinned. Isaac shrugged but grinned back. A bubble of laughter exploded from Spencer and he let it loose and laughed even harder when Isaac joined in.

They'd been out practising to drive for over an hour in the wee hours of the morning. The road was as quiet as it was going to get in London.

"What the hell was that?" Spencer asked, wiping the tears from his eyes with the sleeve of his jumper. He hadn't laughed that hard in years.

Isaac shrugged, but his eyes, so like his father's, held a spark of humour.

"You can parallel park into the tightest of spaces, drive a car like Lewis Hamilton, but don't know your left from right?"

Spencer was only joking, but Isaac frowned and turned to look straight ahead. His knuckles were a pale white as he gripped the steering wheel.

Spencer was silent for a moment, recalling everything that had happened tonight. "Take me home kid," he said finally. "I have a plan."

★★★

"I can't believe you got a tattoo, Dad. And you said I couldn't get one." Gabbriella held both her father's hands in hers and peered through the cling-film that protected the tattoos on the inside of his wrists. "And you too?" She looked over at her brother.

Isaac grinned and held out his own wrists for his sister to examine.

"Both of you? The same thing?"

"Yep," Spencer answered.

It had been a great day. Spencer felt like he'd finally got something right with his son. They'd laughed as they flipped though the huge tattoo books together before Isaac, shaking his head, asked for a pencil and piece of paper and quickly drew what he wanted.

Spencer had added to it and his heart zapped when he saw the look of respect and admiration in his son's eyes. Spencer was a born artist, and he told Isaac about his paintings and the canvas stand Della had bought him for his birthday when he was thirteen. Yes, it had been a good day.

"Della's not going to like this," Gabbriella said, turning away and stuffing her hands into the pockets of her jeans.

"Isaac, why don't you get changed and we'll go out to dinner?"

Spencer watched him walk to the stairs and carefully climb the glass steps. He needed to do something about those damn steps, he silently reminded himself.

"Gabbs?" Spencer whispered to his daughter. When she turned around, he indicated the kitchen with his head.

Gabbriella followed him but folded her arms across her chest as she faced him.

"Remember Isaac told you he couldn't pass his test?"

She nodded.

"He can drive. Very well in fact, but he gets his left and right mixed up."

"So?"

"Watch your tone, young lady," Spencer warned. "So we got tattoos. A lion on the left and the word Rasta with a fist on the right."

"Oh."

"So there's no need for the sulks."

"I wasn't sulking."

Spencer affectionately pinched her bottom lip between his fingers. "Yes you were." He kissed her on the forehead. "You can choose where to go for dinner."

Gabbriella grinned and Spencer could feel his wallet squeeze itself shut in protest.

## CHAPTER TWENTY-EIGHT

The long-staying guests at the sanctuary were only allowed to use letters to communicate with their families and Spencer had been pleasantly surprised when Della wrote to him, inviting him for a visit. The sanctuary was a retreat that ran daytime meditation classes, as well as weekly and monthly mental, physical and verbal retreats. Della had already spent a month in silence. She'd missed Christmas and New Year's.

Spying the simple wooden sign, Spencer turned right and drove down a long bumpy lane with a strip of grass in the middle to find a large stone house with a small fountain at the front. The house had two stories on the right and a single level extension on the left. Postcard ivy crept up the walls. Overall, the house fit in perfectly with the panoramic views of the Peak District.

Getting out of the car, Spencer swung his arms high over his head, stretching the kinks out of his back until he felt a click and breathed in deeply. His nostrils flared and his nose tingled as the fresh cold air swept through his body. It was clean and rejuvenating. Perfect for starting over.

The front door opened and Della stepped out, already dressed for the outdoors in walking boots, coat, hat and gloves.

"Hi," she greeted him.

"Hi."

They looked at each other. Both aware that their relationship had been stripped to its emotional core. Today felt like a first date.

She looked rested, Spencer noted, but her eyes were wary and guarded, as though waiting for him to say something horrible. He never ever wanted her to be wary of him again.

"Did we ever go on a date?" Spencer asked suddenly into the lingering silence. They stood facing each other. Close, but distinctly apart.

"What?"

"Did we ever go on an official date?"

The question left Della puzzled, but seeing the determined glint in his eyes, she decided to humour him.

"We went for pizza in Manor Park."

"No." Spencer shook his head. "There was always a gang of people around when we went there. Besides we'd always gone there. It wasn't anything special."

Della shifted from one foot to the next and shrugged and Spencer realised the movement was similar to Isaac's. Their son. He relaxed into a smile.

"Would you like to go on a date with me?"

"Where?"

Spencer looked around, spying a narrow footpath that disappeared into a wall of trees. "Down there."

Della looked in the direction Spencer was pointing to. She'd taken that path many times this past month, knowing there were rest benches along the way. She didn't know where the path led though. She was advised by the staff to never wander off it.

"Okay."

Spencer held out his arm and she tucked her gloved hand into the bend at his elbow and together they walked down the path.

"We did go on a date you know," she started conversationally.

"I don't think we did," he said. "Primary school doesn't count, and when we got to high school there was always people around. We were never really alone when we went out."

"I guess you're right." Della remembered the crowd that seemed to be always around him, thanks to his popularity.

The path narrowed for a moment and Della let his arm go to walk in front of him.

"We were just—," Spencer searched for the right word and came up with, "together."

"Together." Della repeated, unsure of what to say next and where the conversation was leading.

"History almost repeated itself you know," Spencer said a moment later as they walked into a small clearing.

"What do you mean?"

"Nicole."

"Your daughter?"

"She's pregnant."

Della stumbled and Spencer's hand shot out around her waist to steady her. "Oh Spencer, I'm sorry."

"It's okay. She's going to be okay." Then he added almost fiercely as he stepped away to pick a leaf off a tree looking at it intently, "We're going to be okay."

"The father?"

"Threw her out when she told him." He threw the leaf down and turned to her with a smile. "You've raised a fine young man, Della."

"I know." She smiled confidently. "I'm glad you've had the chance to know him."

"I actually thought Nicole was happily playing house when Isaac told me the truth. The last time I'd spoken to her properly I'd given her an ultimatum and lost. She'd opted for the boyfriend."

"I'm sorry."

"It's my fault." He captured her hand and started swinging it back and forth. "My track record with the women in my life isn't a very good one." The small smile he levelled at her was tinged with sadness. "It was Isaac who basically told me to man up."

"He actually said 'man up'?"

"Practically. We didn't know she was living in a women's shelter, but she and Isaac had been Skyping for a while and she told him."

"He has that effect on people."

"He does," Spencer echoed proudly. He decided now was not the time to tell her Isaac had fallen down the glass staircase and grazed himself so badly that he had to be taken to hospital. They'd packed up and moved back to Nottingham after that. Nicole had come with them.

Della grinned. "You're going to be a granddad," she teased.

"I'm going to be a granddad."

They walked on.

★★★

Spencer was looking out his window at the exact same time Isaac jumped over the fence and sneaked into the house.

"What's in the bag?" Spencer asked, walking into Isaac's bedroom moments later. They'd decided it would be better if Isaac stayed with them until his mother came back or permanently if Spencer had his way. They'd settled into a workable routine and together they'd sorted out his clothes into easy piles and even mapped out his days on a new calender, including chores and father-son time. "What's in the backpack?" he repeated grimly.

"Nothing."

Spencer held out his hand for the black bag with a foreboding feeling. Isaac was dressed in full black, with his hood pulled low over his head, shadowing his eyes. The black bandanna, which was obviously used to cover his nose and mouth, was now pulled down to his chin. He'd been doing something.

"Are you in a gang?"

"No."

"Doing something you shouldn't be doing?"

"No."

"Then what's with the get-up and you sneaking out?"

"Nothing."

"I promised your mother I'd look out for you and that includes keeping you safe and out of trouble."

Isaac stared at him for a long while, and Spencer held his gaze.

"Here." Isaac threw the bag down at Spencer's feet and crossed his arms high over his chest.

Spencer looked down at the backpack. The challenge was on. He knew if he looked in it the trust he and Isaac had built would be ruined. He'd made such a mess of his relationships with his children and was well aware he had to stop the mistrust and the controlling bull-headedness Nicole had accused him of having. Isaac was home and he was safe.

"Don't leave this house again without telling me," Spencer warned before turning and leaving the room.

## CHAPTER TWENTY-NINE

"I quit my job," Spencer announced one evening, as they took a stroll down the same path, on their second date, a week later.

He caught Della as she stumbled, but unlike the last time he didn't let her go. Instead, he pulled her closer until the front of her body was brushing against his.

"Quit?" Della asked.

"Yeah,"he confirmed with a lazy grin. "I'd been thinking about it for some time and what with Gabbs already enrolled at a college in Nottingham." He raised a single brow at her knowingly, aware she had been privy to that little secret for months. "It felt like the right thing to do."

He continued, "I'm still on many boards but officially off the corporate conveyor belt, and it feels damn right."

"But what are you going to do?"

"Whatever."

"That isn't the right attitude to take. You need to set an example," Della said.

"To who?"

"Your girls. Isaac."

He laughed out loud. "They're the ones who instigated it all."

"And they're okay with it?"

"Yes, Della. They're okay with it." Spencer chuckled. "They knew I wasn't happy. I knew there was more to me than the man behind the desk, and I've known for some time." He stopped and pulled her around to him. "But what about you?"

"What about me?"

"I'm here for good," Spencer said.

"I know."

"How do you feel about that?"

"Remember you asked me about our first date and neither of us could figure out when it was? It just was?"

"Yeah."

"This just is."

"That makes no sense."

"Who said it was meant to?"

"Hmm." He started walking. "You're right," he said eventually. "It just is."


"Let's sit here," Della said as they came to a wooden bench weathered to a lovely muted brown.

"Are you warm enough?"

"Hmm hmm." She looked ahead seeing the grassy moors and misty hills in the distance. "I love it here."

"Isaac told me you've been here before."

She turned to him, alarmed. Isaac never mentioned this to her. "He remembered that?"

"He was eleven years and three months, he told me."

She laughed although it was a little off centre.

"It wasn't a good time for me back then."

"Tell me."

"I was lonely. Isaac was growing and getting too much for me to handle. I just wanted to be able to share some of the responsibility." Della laughed. "I guess that was the problem. I didn't put much thought into what I really wanted and who I allowed into our lives."

"Isaac told me what he did."

"Yes."

"It wasn't your fault."

"I know that. Being here has allowed me to think for myself for the first time in years. I've been meditating, reading, asking questions into the silence and getting answers."

She shifted on the bench so that her knees were touching his and she could see his face. "Do you want to know what I asked?"

"Tell me."

"What to do about you."

Spencer sat up stiffly. Did he really want to know? Could Della really find the answer to their relationship after only a couple of weeks? She was here to work on herself.

"And what was the answer?" he asked. She was looking at him expectantly.

"I'd always believed I'd find myself a kingman who had the same beliefs and followed the same moral code as me."

Spencer had to stop his teeth from grinding together. "I'm not a Rasta, Della."

"I know that."

"And don't ever intend to embrace it," he added, his voice darkening.

Della laughed at him affectionately, then reached for his gloved hand and laced her fingers through his.

"You're a Rasta through and through, Spencer."

He let out a laugh as cold and brittle as a sheet of thin ice. "So that's what you've told yourself, is it?" He released her hand and glared at her.

"What do you mean?" Della asked.

"It's okay for you to love me now that I've developed a taste for herbal tea?" He moved away to stand with his back to her.

"Of course not." She walked over to him, touching his arm. "Spencer? What are you talking about?"

"You know what, Della? I don't want to hear it. If you think you

194

can only love me by forcing me to be something I'm not then that's it! Which makes me the damn fool. Again."

She gasped, trying to understand.

"Why are you forcing Rastafarianism on me," Spencer accused, breaking the thickening silence. "When you yourself don't know what you want?"

"Excuse me? And it's not Rastafarianism."

"Whatever."

"Why are you being like this?"

"Because you always want to try and change me into something I'm not. Putting me on some sort of pedestal."

"That's not true, and don't talk to me about pedestals! You're just as guilty!"

"Then why call me your kingman, or whatever it was you said. I'm not a Rasta."

"Spencer, I don't understand why you are so upset. I just said you have Rasta in your heart. That's a good thing. The world needs more people like you."

Spencer felt physically sick as vomit suddenly clogged up his throat. He closed his eyes trying valiantly to will it away.

"Let's go."He grabbed her hand and dragged her along the path.
"But—"

"Don't," Spencer warned. "Don't say a word."

He kissed her at the door, hard but with a wealth of feelings Della couldn't decipher. Spencer then got in his car and drove off.

★★★

Della reached for the door handle behind her and turned the brass knob. She didn't understand what had just happened, what had made Spencer so angry.

The day had started. She'd woken free of all those mixed up feelings of self-doubt and confusion that had shadowed her for so many years. She knew who she was. She didn't need a hair style, dreadlocks or weaves, bald head or braids. She was more than how she looked. Her hair didn't define her. She had looked beyond her reflection and seen herself. Finally, in the weeks of silence, free from distractions and worry, time and noise, she had finally seen the woman she was meant to be.

A car came up the lane, but it wasn't Spencer and she retreated, dejectedly, into the house. The place felt too warm, the walls too close and suffocating. She swung open the door again and retraced their steps up the narrow footpath.

Spencer had found her sitting on the very same bench, with her hat pulled low on her head and her hands in her coat pockets. She didn't look up when he sat beside her.

"I need to tell you what happened to me when you left," he began. "I told you I was a bit lost when you disappeared. Everyone pulling me in every direction. Nobody listening to me but telling me to forget you. I couldn't forget you."

She reached out to touch him.

He jerked away from him. "No don't touch me."

"I went for a drive, up Papine, through Irish Town, way up into the hills. I was hungry and stopped to pick some stringys."

"Strings?"

"Stringy mangos, the ones that get stuck in your teeth and makes a mess,"he explained laughing as the image of the sticky juice trickling down his arms flashed across his mind. "There was so many mangoes hanging in the road, and I remember leaning against the car eating one after the other and hearing water. It was getting dark and I didn't know where I was, but I didn't care. Nothing mattered anymore. I walked until I found the river and took a swim."

He looked at her for a moment, his gaze vacant and dark. Della held her breath, not sure if he was going to go on.

"A man attacked me with a machete."

She gasped, remembering the many scars she'd seen on his body.

"I don't remember much else apart from his crazy eyes and long matted hair. There was a gunshot and I'd past out."

"He shot you?"

"No. Someone chased him off or killed him. They never found

him. Next I know I was in the hospital."

"Thank God."

"You don't get it. I saw the light and I touched it."

"I don't think I understand what you're saying?"

"It doesn't matter," Spencer replied. "It was a long time ago."

"But it's still affecting you. Still affecting us."

"Della, I was given a second chance and took it. I met my wife, married her and had my girls. I forgot about you and got on with my life. You'd taken everything from me and left me for dead."

Della moved away from him. "That's an awful thing to say," she whispered, shocked that he could say such a thing.

"It's the truth," he went on relentlessly. "You were selfish. I was selfish. But I tell you this, I will never be a Rastafarian just because you want me to be. I am me."

"Listen to me!" Della grabbed his face, forcing him to look at her. "Listen to me, Spencer. What I meant is that it doesn't matter who you are or who I am. It's what's in here." She held his hand and put it to her breast.

"Feel my heart beating, Spencer. Feel that rhythm? It's the same as yours."Tears rolled down her cheeks, as she pulled him closer to her, so they were standing and facing each other beside the bench. "I love you. I don't care who you believe in. What matters is that you never leave me again. Spencer please." She hugged him tight, hearing his heartbeat beneath her ear.

"It doesn't matter what I look like. It doesn't matter what you believe in." She sobbed into his jacket. "I'm yours."

Spencer absorbed her words. They penetrated his skin and settled in a tight cluster around his heart. It didn't matter, he convinced himself. They had always loved each other. They had been given a second chance.

Spencer made a step back and tipped her chin so that he could see her beautiful face. Her lovely eyes were awash with tears, and he used his thumbs to wipe them away.

"I love you," she whispered earnestly as though saying it for the very first time. This time the words mattered. This time she really felt them in her heart.

He nodded and bent to kiss her softly on the lips. They stood, locked in a tight embrace, feeling the bond that had always been there.

"I love you exactly as you are, Spencer," she stated with utter conviction. She had to make him believe her.

When they'd met up again all those months ago, they hadn't cleared the air, too busy scrambling around and shoving their lives together to make things work. They'd been fitting there lives together, pretending all was well. But this was their new beginning.

Della had been as much a victim as he was. They'd been forced apart and manipulated by people who didn't grasp the depth of feelings they had for each other. Some people spend their whole lives never finding that mirror image of themselves. Spencer and Della had found it as children. And it was as beautiful as it was rare.

Spencer sighed and placed his forehead against hers, unable to speak. He was too overcome with emotion. Instead of saying another word, he pulled her over to the bench and settled her tenderly in his lap.

## CHAPTER THIRTY

"We got you a house-warming gift, Della," Gabbs said, barely able to contain her excitement as she looked at her watch then out of the window.

They were at Della's terrace house, now lavishly decorated with helium balloons and a hand-painted welcome home banner Isaac had made.

"Another one?"

"This one is well peng, Della. Stay there!" she yelled. The doorbell rang.

"Isaac, you answer the door,"Gabbs ordered.

"You answer the door," her brother teased without moving.

"I'll answer the door,"Nicole offered, getting to her feet and smoothing her hand over her slight bump. Della caught herself frequently staring at Nicole whose resemblance to Isaac was startling. They could have been twins.

"Close your eyes, Della," said Gabbs. "Open them now."

"Spencer?"As thrilled as Della was to see him, his appearance came as no surprise. He'd only gone out to pick up some groceries about half an hour earlier. Spencer stepped to the side to reveal her darling Mr. Motive, scratching his neck and making the bell on his collar jingle.

Della sprang to her feet, grabbed him up. Ignoring the meow of his protest, she hugged him close. She hadn't seen him in months and she buried her nose in his grey fur.

"Oh, Mr. Motive," she cried.

"Why are you crying?"Isaac asked, frowning at his mother.

"They're just silly tears." Della sniffed. She'd really missed her cat.

"OMG, OMG. Oh. My. God!"Gabbriella yelled, looking at her new iPad.

"What?" they asked in unison.

"I've got 8089 followers on my Instagram!"

★★★

"Come on," Spencer said sometime later after they'd had a light lunch and Isaac had played a song for them on his guitar. "We'd best get going. Della needs to rest."

"No, I don't," she protested

"You do. We left Bakewell pretty early, and these guys haven't let you come up for air."

"I like it."

He smiled at her tenderly. "I know you do."

"Do you want us to go into another room so you can get your freaky on, Dad?" asked Gabbs mischievously.

"Gabbriella!"

"What? I'm only saying what everyone else was thinking."

Della looked around her pretty little room, knowing it would feel as empty as the fridge when they all left.

"Can I come with you?"

This was huge, Spencer knew. This wasn't her asking if she could come round for a cup of tea. She wanted to be part of his family. He grinned. In fact, he'd been grinning ever since they had that talk on the bench in the middle of the Peak District.

Della had decided to stay and finish her programme and he had settled his family in Nottingham.

"Put her bags in the car, guys. She's coming home with us."

Della looked down at the cat in her lap, not wanting to leave him again so soon.

"Maybe I'd better stay and get him settled first?"

"Oh no, Della. He's been living with us," Gabbs revealed. "Dad couldn't stand the thought of the poor little guy being stuck in that cattery when we had a perfectly good home for him, didn't you Dad?"

Della laughed loving the big softy even more. And she didn't mean the cat.

*** 

Spencer looked into the room. He'd never been so happy. Everyone talking at once, talking over each other and trying to be heard. Gabbriella winning every time.

They'd just finished eating the dinner Nicole had cooked. She'd always been a good cook and had gone out with Della to buy a vegetarian cookbook in town.

Yes, Spencer was happy.

"What are you thinking about?" Della wrapped her arms around his waist and looked up at him. She'd notice the pensive look on his face as he leaned in the doorway, watching them all.

"Taking you to bed."

"No, you weren't."

"No, I wasn't," he admitted.

"Look at them." He turned her around so that her back was leaning against his chest and together they looked at their children. Isaac was strumming his new guitar; Gabbs was taking a picture of him doing it and Nicole was baking. It was a picture-perfect scene of family life.

"One person is missing."

"I know."

"Shall we see if we can get her on Skype?"

"Nah. She's busy going off on Safari with the Ali's."

"Sure?"

"Yeah."

"Your hair is really soft," Spencer said, rubbing his chin over her short hair.

"Hmm hmm. Or maybe it's just your bristles?

"Bristles? Who even uses that word anymore?"

Della laughed and made her way to the stairs, stopping momentarily to throw him a sultry look over her shoulder. "Coming?"

\*\*\*

"You can't go on like this."

"Like what?" Spencer asked.

"Staying at home playing your stupid records day in and day out. You need to get out of the house and earn a living."

"I don't need to."

"Everyone needs a purpose, no matter how much money they have. This is unhealthy. The girls are worried."

"I'm fine, resting. This is my form of retreat."

"I don't think so, Spencer," Della countered.

He crossed his arms over his chest. "So what do you propose?"

"I don't know."

"Let me know when you do."

"Oh, for goodness sake."

"Are you happy?" he asked her suddenly.

"Blissfully."

He reached for her hand and kissed it. "Are you bored?"

"No, yes, sometimes. Why?"

"Nothing, really. I know you liked working."

"Not really. That was my job. I had no aspirations to go any further than I was. I didn't want the responsibility."

"It surprised me to see you there, but that was before I knew about

Isaac and the sacrifices you made."

"It wasn't a sacrifice; it's just what you do when you're a single parent. You get on with it."

"I know. I got on with it, with the girls. But at least I didn't have any money worries. Time, yes. Money, no," Spencer offered.

"I didn't really either. It was easy enough with just the two of us. I only went out to work when he went to school full-time. And then when he got the flat I upped my hours and switched shifts so I could be there if he needed me during the day."

"You did a great job."

Della smiled and they looked at each other for a long moment.

"Did you know he can draw?"

"Just like you," she confirmed.

"Yeah, just like me."

"And he has tattoos. Just like you."

"Yeah, just like me."

"You're lucky I'm not mad at you both."

"I know."

"Spencer?"

"Hmm hmm." He pulled her onto his knee to nuzzle her neck. "You smell so good."

"There's something you should know."

"Oh yeah." He stopped nibbling on her ear. "Are you pregnant?"

"What? No." Della slid off his lap. "I can't have anymore children. They tied my tubes right after I had the twins because of the difficulties I had during the pregnancy." She eyed him anxiously. They'd never talked about more children. "Does it matter?"

He caught her by the hand again and yanked her slight figure back onto his lap. "No, of course not."

He went back to nuzzling her neck and creeping his hand under her jumper. "My hands are full with my three beautiful daughters, a talented son, a headstrong Rasta woman and a grandchild on the way and a moody cat. My life is complete."

## CHAPTER THIRTY-ONE

"Della!" Mac yelled from across the room as soon as Della stepped through the double doors.

It was her first time at the office since the stabbing and she'd been feeling pretty guilty for not working her notice and saying goodbye.

Although Spencer had withdrawn from day-to-day duties with the group of companies, he'd arranged this visit for her as a surprise.

"Oh my God, Della, you look so different!" Lucia exclaimed, pulling Della close so that she could touch her head now covered with about half an inch of soft tight curls.

Della smiled and dipped her head so Lucia could get better access. To her, the Pod Eight lot was like family so she didn't object as Lucia's smoothed her hands over her curls.

"I love it," Lucia declared, reaching into a small box beside her monitor that held a few personal things. "I made these." She held out a pair of large orange and brown beaded earrings. "They'd look great with your new hair cut."

"Thank you, sweetheart." Della hugged her close, accepting the earrings.

"Luckily you have a nice head, Della. I'd look like a frigging cracked egg!" Fliss joked as she cut off her customer and punched in a random code so that she could move around the pod to hug her friend. Della was the only one she touched freely.

"Aww, Fliss, I've missed you so." Della hugged her fiercely. "How are you?"

"You know how it is," Fliss replied, looking at the floor.

"Did you get my text message with my new address?"

"Yeah."

"Why didn't you answer it?"

"No credit." Fliss bit her lip

"Answer my texts, Felicity," Della ordered gently.

"I will."

"Where is everyone?" Della asked, looking around. Members of the other night teams waved and she waved back.

"Ingrid has the night off and Pryia is on her break."

Just then Monica-Louise came onto the floor.

"Della! Lovely to see you!"

Della almost didn't recognise her. She'd lost weight, got rid of the bad hair extensions and dyed her hair.

"You look great."

"So do you," Monica replied, before turning to Fliss. "I see you've signed yourself out."

Felicity looked warily at the team captain, biting her tongue to stop the barrage of insults that were ready to tumble out. She'd been trying really hard to control her temper and her language.

"Use the meeting code and I'll exception it for you."

Fliss's mouth dropped open in shock, but she quickly did as she was told. She didn't know what had been going on with the team captain but she'd been a lot nicer to her lately and even recommended she join one of the many employee programmes going on. "Thanks."

Monica-Louise dipped her head in acknowledgement. "Okay everyone, since our mother is here," she said and winked at Della, "I'll re-route the calls for ten minutes."

There was a chorus of whoops. Headsets hit the desks and chairs were rolled backwards as they all descended on Della.

"So who won that Christmas competition?" Della asked a few minutes later, remembering all the extra sales they'd managed to get.

"Them lot."Jared nodded towards the other pod.

"They won by 1.34 percent,"Monica-Louise told her.

"Oh, so close. I'm sorry."

"No, don't be." Mac grabbed Della's arm. "I was right. Benidorm was first prize," he said, with a dramatic shudder. They all laughed.

"Can you imagine him in Benidorm?" Fliss added.

"Don't, Fliss. It doesn't bear thinking about." He rolled his eyes. He gave Della a quick hug, made a call-me sign with his hand, and went to use his mobile.

Seeing Monica-Louise look at her precious screens, Della said a tearful goodbye and closed another chapter in her life.

Spencer was waiting for her in the car park listening to music. The sound of Beres Hammond's rich voice spilled into the night air when she opened the car door.

"Okay?"

"Yep."

"Where to?"

"Home." Della took a deep breath. "I need to speak to my mother."

* * *

Della's mobile went off and then Spencer's three seconds later. They both reached for them and sat bolt upright, seeing the white-gloved thumbs down, the unhappy smiley face and crying smiley face on their respective screens.

"Oh, my God!" Della screeched.

"Where is he?"

"I don't know."

Spencer, springing out of bed, pulled on his jeans and ran into Isaac's room. It was empty.

"Ring him. He can't send us a message like that!"

"What is it, Dad?" Nicole said sleepily from her bedroom door.

206

"Isaac. He sent us his distress signal."

"What do you mean?"

"I can't explain right now."

Della came onto the landing dressed in jeans and a jumper.

"Did you get him?"

She nodded.

"Well?"

"He's at the police station."

"What? What did he do?"

"I don't know."

"You stay here with your sister," he told Nicole. "And try not to get upset. It's not good for the baby."

Spencer headed for his room, dragged on a jumper and socks and trainers and met Della at the front door.

"I can go if you want to stay," he offered, noting how pinched she looked.

"No, it's okay." She put her hand on his arm. "I'm just glad you're here with me."

"Come on. Tell me where to go."

***

At the police station they had to press the button to the intercom and identify themselves before they were buzzed through.

Isaac was sitting on a bench with his head tipped back against the wall with his eyes closed. Della rushed over to him.

"Are you okay?"

He nodded, but kept his eyes closed.

"Della, the lights," Spencer said. "Where's your glasses?"

"They took them."

Spencer approached the waist high counter and slammed his palm on the surface.

"My son can't see without his glasses," he yelled, spying several uniformed policemen through a glass door chatting and drinking tea.

An older officer with a pot belly and greying hair came forward.

"They aren't prescription."

"He has light sensitivity," Spencer explained. "He can't see without them."

"Right," The officer replied, but felt under the counter anyway and handed Isaac's glasses to him.

Isaac wiped his eyes with his sleeve before putting them on, blinking several times before opening his eyes properly.

"What is he charged with?"

"Vandalism."

"Don't be stupid," Spencer returned. "Isaac wouldn't do that."

"Right," the officer drawled. "Ask him where we picked him up?"

Spencer turned to his son.

"Did you vandalise something?"

"No."

"He said he didn't and I believe him."

"Well, isn't that nice," the officer scoffed turning to his colleague who had joined him. "A parent who doesn't believe their kid could commit a crime. Look, he'll be sleeping here tonight, mate."

"Now, wait a minute," Spencer balled his fists and leaned over the counter. "I am not your mate."

"Spencer," Della warned softly, putting her hand on his arm to calm him down.

"No. He's coming home with us," Spencer stated adamantly. "Have you charged him with anything?"

"You don't get it mate, he's violent," the officer said with a flicker of irritation. "This isn't his first, second or third offence. He's known to us. We've got him on CCTV. Again. Defacing the city. Again."

Both officers moved around the counter and pulled Isaac to his feet.

"Get your hands off my son!" Spencer yelled, stepping forward as Isaac tried to shrug them off.

"Spencer!" Della cried in alarm as she watched with disbelief as Spencer was wrestled to the ground.

Spencer hit his head and for a moment he was by the river trying to protect himself from the lethal machete that was being swung at him.

He heard Della scream and he shook his head to clear it.

"Are you going to behave yourself Sir?" The officer asked as he removed his knee from Spencer's back and pulled him to his feet.

Spencer nodded."Sorry."

He was released and Spencer watched as Isaac's hands were cuffed behind his back with a white cable tie.

"As I was saying," the senior officer said again. "He's known to us."

"It's not what you think," Della whispered through guilty tears.

"Tell me what I'm thinking," Spencer invited coldly, his eyes darkening as he looked at her. The boy was a criminal. Violent. A Rastafarian he'd allowed near his daughters'.

Della shivered. "Not now, Spencer, please," she begged. "We need to get him some help."

Spencer sucked in some much-needed air before turning back to the officer. He'd do this one thing for her and that would be it.

"What do we need to do?"

★★★

Della looked out at the people seated in rows on the white plastic chairs in their newly landscaped garden.

It had turned out beautifully. The weather was favourable and touched by the fragrance of pink spring blossoms. Perfect for the biggest day of their lives.

Spencer was on the stage, talking with such passion and enthusiasm to their two hundred guests of reporters, local MPs, The Sheriff of Nottingham, parents and children from the centre and many more who had come out to support Isaac and his cause. There wasn't a dry eye left in the place.

It had been a chaotic few months and they'd all been severely tested, almost losing Isaac in a system that didn't understand the problems dyspraxics and their carers faced was perhaps the biggest test of all.

The national Save Isaac Campaign was born, the result of their hard work in raising awareness and Spencer ringing and emailing everyone including the Prime Minister in Jamaica who contacted the High Commissioner in London. Not to mention a whisper to the newspapers.

Then there was the campaign by the Arts Council to save the works of pavement art Isaac had done across Nottingham and a call to allow him to finish the lamppost he'd started in London.

Isaac had become a local hero and a national treasure, but he took it all in stride. Anyone else would have been uncomfortable seated on a stage with the young prince, who was also sporting a pair of Isaac's trademark tinted glasses. Isaac turned to Della and winked before looking across at Casey, his now ex-support worker in the front row. He winked at her too.

Della was overjoyed to see her friends from Pod Eight, including Mackenzie, Felicity, Pryia and Ingrid, all in the second row. Monica-Louise and Jarrett were on the other side of the aisle, with the rest of the night teams, a sprinkling of the day teams and The Steel Lions.

Nicole sat at the end of the front row, her bump more pronounced, looking beautifully radiant. She was scheduled to start a cookery course in the summer at the university.

Gabbriella was beside her, taking pictures of her brother and the prince for her Instagram, while trying to catch the prince's eye at the same time.

Ras Simeon gave her mother, who had flown in for the event, a handkerchief and Della watched as she dabbed elegantly at her tears and blushed at something Ras Simeon had said. He and Spencer were now firm friends and Spencer had even hosted one of their reasoning sessions.

Spencer reached the end of his speech and named the amount they'd raised for the Dyspraxic Society. The spring air exploded with the sounds of cheers, clapping and high-fives. Even the prince and the High Commissioner high-fived everyone on stage.

Spencer turned to beam at Della, the love flowing easily between them. They'd celebrated her birthday privately that morning. Della touched the eternity ring on her left hand, remembering the 'Just is' inscription.

Della's heart was so full she could barely contain her happy tears again. And there, walking towards them through the crowd, was another image of Spencer. Jesse was home.

# ABOUT THE AUTHOR

When I described myself to my friends I called myself an introvert and they laughed so hard I should really be offended.

I consider myself to be very lucky as although born in Britain, I spent my formative years mostly in Kingston Jamaica with a long detour through Toronto and Nairobi. I married my college sweetheart David, have two amazing kids, a rabbit and a cat who we live with. I've come full circle and live in Nottingham, just 12 miles from where I was born.

I've also donned the 'headset' and worked in Customer Services firstly with an international flower company (being voted agent of the year worldwide) to working nights talking to overseas customers. Hence this novel has been knocking around in my head for a number of years.

Call Me Royal has become the first book in my Call Centre Series. Look out for Call Me Lucky, Fliss's story coming soon.

To keep up with me and my projects I'm on most of the social media platforms although active on some more than others.

Caroline. X

Facebook: Caroline Bell Foster
Twitter: @cbellfoster
Website: Caroline@carolinebellfoster.com

OTHER TITLES:

LADIES JAMAICA (LMH)
CARIBBEAN WHISPERS (LMH)
SAFFRON'S CHOICE (LMH)
CALL ME LUCKY (SP) – January 2015